Imagination is the station

Where the train of life begins,

It's the ocean where the notion

Of a talking fish can swim,

It's this and that, and that and this,

Not exactly what it seems,

It's that place inside your mind

Where you can manufacture dreams!

The Adventures of
Rupert Starbright
Book 1

THE DOOR
TO FAR-MYST

Mike DiCerto

THE DOOR TO FAR-MYST
© 2011 by Michael Dicerto
ISBN 978-1-936144-68-6
Cover art © Brad W. Foster
Cover design © Chris Cartwright

"Zumaya Thresholds" and the dodo colophon are trademarks of Zumaya Publications LLC, Austin TX.

Look for us online at
http://www.zumayapublications.com

Library of Congress Cataloging-in-Publication Data

DiCerto, Michael, 1965-
  The door to Far-Myst / Michael DiCerto.
      p. cm.
  ISBN 978-1-936144-68-6 (trade pbk. : alk. paper) -- ISBN 978-1-936144-98-3 (electronic/multiple format) -- ISBN 978-1-61271-031-0 (electronic/epub)
  I. Title.
  PZ7.D546Do 2011
  [Fic]--dc23
                                        2011022905

For Valentina, Jillian and William

Three sparkling little humans who call me "Crazy Uncle Mike." I hope this book helps to inspire them to not seek the easy paths but the paths of wonder.

Imagination

is more important than

knowledge.

— *Albert Einstein*

Chapter 1

A Grand Bagoon

A great gust of chilly wind greeted Rupert as he stepped from his house and onto the walk. The crunch under his feet told of a heavy nighttime fall of leaves.

His gray-and-white rake perched on his shoulder, he stepped to the curb and glanced up and down The Curving Road. Other children were already up and raking. Rupert hated raking leaves, but it was of great importance to the adults of Graysland.

He let his head fall back to enjoy the cool breeze that scampered across his street. That's when he saw the strange object in the sky. It was like a giant leaf bag filled with air, but had none of the dull, faded colors his eyes were used to. These colors seemed to be alive, pulsing like fire. They made him squint.

1

The object drifted high above the trees, a few blackbirds nosily flying around it for a look. It moved west and sank slowly, and he saw a swirling pattern on its round surface made up of a mixture of unknown shades.

Some of the colors seemed hot, while others appeared as cold as the coldest winter day. Some of them screamed out like a grumpy baby while others seemed to sing with a wonderful feeling of peace. A few reminded Rupert of the way certain fruits tasted.

He dropped his rake and stepped out into the middle of The Curving Road, his eyes never leaving the thing. It was a monster—as large as two houses.

"Squeem! Look at this!"

Squeem, his best friend, was a short, somewhat flabby boy with hair the exact same shade as a winter sky. He looked up from his raking.

"What's the matter, Rupert? You lose a leaf in a gust?"

A scream turned Rupert's head. His mother stood in the doorway of their house with her mouth open so wide one of the nosy blackbirds could have flown in and nested quite comfortably.

"Rupert! Get inside at once! Don't look at that!" Olga screamed.

Rupert wasn't scared by her warnings. He was too busy looking at the amazing sight.

Squeem, rake still in hand, stepped up beside him and gazed where Rupert was looking. His mouth fell open even wider than Olga's.

"Wow."

More screams filled the air on the normally quiet street as more parents emerged from their homes to see what the fuss was about. They watched in fear as the floating thing shifted direction and headed south, up and over the nearby hillside.

Rupert's heart pounded, and a strange feeling filled his body. He was fascinated by this object. He had to see it up close.

His rake clanged on the asphalt as he let it fall. He took off down the road faster than he had ever run before. Squeem's rake clanged, too, and he followed. The adults on The Curving Road screamed some more, but not one of them chased after the two daring boys.

All over town, as the balloon passed, rakes went clanging onto the streets and sidewalks as children ran. Parents screamed in horror. For the first time ever in Graysland, many, many rakes lay unattended and many leaves were left to blow in the breeze.

There were nothing but open fields of dirt and prickly shrubs on No Homes Avenue. Three dozen or so kids had gathered, many of them still out of breath from chasing the floating thing.

Hanging from the great air-filled ball was a basket made of thick braided wicker, which Rupert could see as the balloon came to rest in a field full of old paving stones and weeds. In the basket stood a man with a beard that hung down to his waist, its color another Rupert had never seen before. And his clothes—well, they were a spectacle all by themselves.

His clothes fluttered in the slightest breeze like a flock of birds. From the toes of his striped boots to the top of his tassel-covered stove-pipe hat, he was

3

ablaze in colors that had never existed in Rupert's world.

The bearded man unlatched a door on the basket and stepped out, waving and beaming a smile.

"I greet you, children of Graysland! My name is Pie O'Sky, and this is my Grand Bagoon!" the bearded man said in a voice filled with a sparkly sound very different from the bland drone of all the adults Rupert knew. His voice was like water flowing over rocks in a stream. Or like the wind through trees that had all their leaves. The man's voice seemed to have more than just a sound. It had a taste, a feel and a smell.

"Who among you has the greatest imagination?"

Like falling dominoes, expressions of utter confusion fell over the faces of the gathered kids. Hulis Brugla, a tall, skinny lad with large teeth, stepped forward.

"What is imaja dination? Is it a new kind of rake?"

"Imaja dination? Rake?" Pie O'Sky repeated with a smile. "The word is *imagination*, and the one of you with the greatest shall take a wondrous trip!"

A chorus of confusion filled the air. Pie O'Sky stroked his long beard and looked at their baffled expressions. He smiled wider and held up his hands.

"What is imagination, you ask? Well, gather around, my kiddies, and let me explain."

The children formed an imperfect circle, and the bearded man with the odd clothes made his way to the center. He cleared his throat, produced a shiny pitch pipe and blew a note. There were gasps, chuckles and sounds of surprise. He then began to sing.

Imagination is the station
Where the train of life begins,
It's the ocean where the notion
Of a talking fish can swim,
It's this and that, and that and this,
Not exactly what it seems,
It's that place inside your mind
Where you can manufacture dreams!

"Well, that's not boring," Rupert said with a wide-eyed smile. Pie O'Sky winked at him and continued the song.

Do you want to roam the sky
Like a flying pumpkin pie?
Or swim in streams of butter cream
As a yellow dragonfly?
Would it be odd to be a frog
Who travels out in space?
Or to share a cookie with a clock
With gumdrops on its face?

The kids just stared, stunned into silence. Pie O'Sky seemed disappointed that there was no applause but smiled wider and continued with his song.

I can take you to a place
Where there's no such hue as gray!
Elephants are blue and gold,
If you prefer your 'phants that way!
It's a place where "It can't be"
Is something never said.
It's a place where all the colors
Start inside your head!

5

"Where is this place?" Vena Krug wondered.

"Far-Myst!" Pie O'Sky said, folding his arms.

"Far-Myst?" repeated a number of voices.

"Far-Myst!" confirmed the bearded man. "Far-Myst has imagination dripping off the trees like sweet sap. It flows in great rivers and coats everything as far as the eye can see like a fresh snowfall. There is so much imagination you have to kick it out of your path when you walk down the street!"

"Like leaves?" Squeem wondered.

"Like ultra-berry, super-merry, color-blasting, ever-lasting wild and wily leaves!"

"Do you have to rake it twice a day?" Vena asked with a frown of disappointment.

"No. There are no rakes in Far-Myst. Unless, of course, you imagine one," Pie O'Sky said. "I would like to invite the one of you with the best imagination to come with me to Far-Myst as my special guest."

Hushed tones of excitement and utter fear washed over the children of Graysland.

"But we don't have imagination!" someone shouted.

"Our parents would never let us!"

"I still don't know what imagination is!" cried someone else.

"How can we know who has the best something if we don't even know where to find such a something?" Squeem wondered aloud.

"Excellent question," Pie O'Sky said, patting Squeem on the head. "I will put you to the test."

He stepped up to the bagoon's basket and took from it a wooden door in a frame. It was like most of the doors in Graysland, although it was painted bright red and had shiny golden hinges and a large, polished gold knob and plate around its keyhole. He set it down before his audience and gestured dramatically.

"This, my imaginationless young'uns, is a door."

Vena rolled her eyes. "We can see that."

"Oh, can you? But can you see a way to open this door? I do not have the key. It will be up to you to come up with a suitable replacement."

"Why bother?" Rupert said, folding his arms. "All you have to do is walk around it."

"Well, you can if you're a boring, pumpkin-faced banana! On the other hand, going around the door will simple take you to the other side of the door," Pie O'Sky said, demonstrating. "It will not take you to Far-Myst. One must step *beyond* this door, not just through it."

"Why can't you just take us there in your bal-loon?"

"That's *bagoon*. Because, my wise-nosed friend, this is my test. I will give you two days. Two days to imagine. Two days to create a clever solution. Two days to dream up a way to open this door and visit Far-Myst."

All these curious words bounded around their confused little minds: *create, clever, dream, imagine, Far-Myst*.

Their thoughts were rudely interrupted by a screeching, frightened voice.

"Vena Krug, you get home right this minute!"

All faces turned to a bony-faced woman. Velkra Klug stood amid a pack of parents. Some held

7

rakes. Others waved fists and scowled angrily. All of them were wide-eyed and scared.

Vena rushed to her mother, bubbling over with excitement.

"Mom! If I can find an imagination I can go to Far-Myst with Pie O'Sky!"

"Home! Right now!"

Velkra grabbed Vena by the wrist and dragged her off down the road. Other parents sought out their own as the kids moaned and protested.

Pie O'Sky stood back and smiled at the show. He picked up the door-in-the-frame and strolled back to the basket on his bagoon and stepped aboard.

"In two days, kiddies, I will return. Two days! When the fat-faced moon is overhead. Dream away! Dream away!"

The Grand Bagoon gently lifted off the ground.

Rupert never moved as the wondrous spectacle rose ever higher until it vanished into a gathering fog.

Chapter 2

The "I" Word

"Not in a million years, Mr. Rupert Dullz. Not even in five million."

Rupert's father waved his fist in the air to help make his point. Rupert, sitting on the edge of his bed, rested his chin in his palms like an egg in a cup.

"But, Dad, no one from Graysland has been to Far-Myst."

"Nor have any of us been to the underside of a compost heap. I will not have a son of mine associate with horrid demons who fall from the sky like poison rain."

"Pie O'Sky isn't poison rain!"

Polgus Dullz smiled briefly then sat beside Rupert and rested one of his doughy hands on his son's shoulder.

"Rupert, this creature—his strange balloon. All of those terrible shades. It is all very unnatural!"

"Where Pie O'Sky comes from its all color. Colors and imagination. And it's a *bagoon*, Dad, not a balloon."

"Bagoon, balloon, fashnoon," Polgus sneered. "Imagination? What good can something be if we have never heard of it before?"

Rupert's face lit up, and he jumped to his feet.

"It can make pies fly and frogs go into outer space."

"And what good would that do? Frogs in space? And as for pies, I prefer mine sliced and sitting on my plate like pies are suppose to do."

"It can do more. Imagination can do anything."

"*Any*thing is a *dangerous* thing, boy. I've sold many a coffin for folks who toyed with *anything*."

"It's not dangerous. All I need to do is figure out how to open the door. I have two days."

Polgus stood up and wobbled. He always got dizzy when he stood up too fast.

"You have two days to get some sense back in your head. I catch you within two miles of that balloon, and your backside will become a few new shades."

Polgus huffed and puffed and wiped a quart of sweat from his forehead with his shirtsleeve then stormed out of the room. Rupert plopped back down on the bed and stared at the door. His forehead was wrinkled like corduroy pants.

"It's a bagoon!" he repeated.

He fell back onto his bed and stared at the ceiling. *A door with a lock, but a lock with no key.* Where can the key be? Rupert pondered the puzzle until he had to rub his temples with his palms to keep his brain from exploding.

A terrible coughing noise interrupted his thoughts. His grandmother Folka was having another fit of the coffus. Rupert got up and paced. He hated to hear her cough. He placed his ear against the wall and listened as she hacked and hocked and coughed some more. He frowned and left his room.

"Grandma?" he whispered as he tapped gingerly on her door. "Are you okay?"

A soft, tired voice fought against the coughing.

"Come in, Rupert."

He entered as quietly as the creaky hinges would allow. The bed was empty. His grandmother sat in an old creaky rocker, and the slight breeze that squeezed through the poor excuse for a window made the top of her hair dance.

She was a hefty woman, short and squat. With her gray blanket drawn around her, she looked like a baked potato, her snow-white mop of hair a dollop of sour cream. Her face was like the road map of a busy city, with a great collection of lines and wrinkles surrounding her warm eyes and a smile that was at once happy and sad.

She turned to him and cleared her chest with a few more hacking coughs before she managed to say "Hello, Rupert."

"Do you want some dripsludge? Maybe it would help," Rupert offered, picking up the large glass bottle of horrible gook.

"Oh, I think I have had enough dripsludge in my life. Thanks for thinking of me, though."

Rupert offered her a poor excuse for a smile and stepped closer.

"What's the matter?" she asked him. "You lose your real smile on the way in here?"

He shrugged and wasn't sure what to say. Folka extended her withered hand and placed it gently atop his.

"What's wrong? My ears may be old, but they can still hear an angry father, even through solid brick."

"Have you ever been to Far-Myst?"

"I never heard of such a place."

"It's a place that has a lot of imagination."

Folka mouthed the strange word a couple of times before giving way to another coughing fit. Rupert stood by, feeling uncomfortable, and after a moment, she cleared her throat with a wet, gurgling sound. She looked up to him.

"Imagination?" she repeated, as if trying to recall the word like a long-forgotten face in a crowd.

"It's something that can make weird things happen. Funny things. Like turn the ocean into butter cream or stick gum on a clock's face and stuff."

"Well, that is odd." Her smile twisted and widened, and she got lost in her memories for a moment. Then she smiled again. "Imagination. Yes…"

She closed her eyes to gather the old memories.

"When I was a young girl, I spent the summer with my auntie and uncle who lived in the southern hills of Graysland. It was time for the noon raking. I was looking around the basement for a leaf bag when I came across a strange book

"It was not a schoolbook or a book of telephone numbers or a catalog of leaf-collecting accessories. It was what my auntie Broga called a *storybook*, and she got very upset when I showed it to her."

"A storybook?" Rupert wondered.

"She said it was written by the mysterious old man who had lived in the house before them. He had a peculiar name—Mookie Starbright."

"That's definitely not a boring name like Rupert Dullz," Rupert decided.

"She had found many of the storybooks hidden in closets and under floorboards. She said they were dangerous and had to be burned."

"Wow."

"My uncle Nobby took me aside that night and said these storybooks were written just because."

"Just because why?" Rupert didn't understand.

"Just because just because. Mookie Starbright created stories about things that had never really happened."

"If imagination could make fish fly or launch frogs into space, I bet it can easily make just-because stories about stuff that never happened," Rupert said with growing excitement.

"Maybe it could, indeed. Anyway, they insisted there would be no more talk about such nonsense as stories and storybooks and old Mookie Star-bright. And especially, there would be no talk of *imagination*."

"Maybe imagination could even open a locked door without a key," Rupert said as a real smile found his mouth. "And maybe...maybe it could even help you with—"

Folka began coughing again. Rupert decided not to finish his sentence. Instead, he wished his grandmother goodnight and left the room.

13

Rupert tossed and turned all night. His mind raced as fast as he and Squeem had run chasing down the Grand Bagoon of Pie O'Sky.

He thought about the strange old man with the coolest name he had ever heard—Mookie Starbright. Just like old Mookie, he would think of a way to use imagination. And if he did open the door, if he did go to the colorful world of Far-Myst, certainly he would find a way to cure his grandmother of the coffus!

Pie O'Sky and his special door to Far-Myst was all the buzz around Rupert's neighborhood, and an even bigger sensation at school the next day. All the kids gathered to discuss the puzzle where their worried parents couldn't hear.

Mrs. Drumpsitter forbade her fifth-grade class to even mention such things as weirdly colored balloons, oddly dressed strangers who descended from the sky and, especially, the I-word. No one was to even spell I-M-A-G-I-N-A-T-I-O-N, let alone discuss such nonsense. They were to focus their minds on the subject at hand—the history of storage cabinets.

Mrs. Drumpsitter was busy scribbling important dates on the blackboard. Hiding behind the squeaks of the chalk were whispers around the classroom. Notes were passed. Sketches drawn. The minds of Rupert and his classmates were busier than they had been in a long time.

A secret meeting was set. The kids would gather and compare ideas. Compare plans each had concocted to open Pie O'Sky's door.

Huge mountains of leaves sat like giant bison on the open lots of the East Graysland Leaf Processing Plant. These leaf piles would have been the envy of any kid who had ever dived, jumped and wrestled in piles of fallen foliage. They were a hundred feet high and covered with thin netting to protect them from the wind.

They awaited being placed in the great fire chambers — deeply buried pits where all the leaves gathered from all over Graysland were burned in never-ending fires that created steam that powered lights and heated homes.

Rupert, Squeem Bissel, Hulis Brugla, Vena Krug and ten or so others stood outside the main fence that caged the leaf piles. They huddled in the chilly air. The sun was just a dim light beneath the haze of clouds and smoke from the burning leaves that billowed from the tops of great smokestacks like giant cigars.

"It's easy," Hulis said with perfect confidence. "All we need is a huge log. Do like they used to do to the castle walls in olden times. We just bust right through it!"

A noisy mixture of moans and shouts of approval erupted. Tweekus Borm, an axe-faced boy with greasy hair who lived on The Easy Road, the richest street in all of Graysland, stepped up.

"My father is the number-one keymaker in all of Graysland. He has a trunk in our attic with a million hundred keys. One of them will open this door. Did you notice the keyhole? It was a primitive model. Probably a standard SK-one hundred."

Again, more moans and shouts.

Through it all, Rupert said nothing. As ideas were tossed about, none seemed to have the imagination Pie O'Sky had sung about. Even though he was still rather unsure what that word meant, he could feel it in his bones—none of the solutions seemed right.

"There's no way my mother's gonna let me out at night to go see that bagoon," Vena said with a scowl.

"Me, neither," Squeem agreed.

There were more shouts and moans. All the shouting and moaning were making Rupert's ears throb. He cleared his throat and stepped forward.

"You're all eating a lot of air and giving me a headache. Pie O'Sky said to meet him in two days, when the moon was overhead. That's what I'm going to do. Anyone who wants to join me, meet me on the corner of The Curving and Bee Line. Tonight. When the moon is overhead. Bring a jacket, a flash-lamp and a way to open that door. And be quiet when you're sneaking out. We don't need a bunch of nosy parents making a mess of things."

With that, he marched home as more moans and shouts erupted.

It was ten minutes past nine, and the moon was climbing the sky slowly but surely, the way moons like to do. In his bed, Rupert lay on his back, his hands clasped behind his head. He knew that when the moon peeked in through his tiny window it would be time to leave.

Beside him sat a collection of items he was positive he would need once he had successfully entered the Land of Far-Myst—a flash-lamp, a candle, a woolen hat, gloves, a package of stone-flour crackers, a half-empty jar of pickle-berry butter, a hunk of stinkcheese, two almost rotten pears, a lump of sugar that had hardened in the bottom of the sugar bowl, a roll of toilet paper, a change of underwear, a facecloth, a stick, a rock, a package of matches and a photo of him with his grandma. All of these items were wrapped inside his jacket, the sleeves tied together to form a handle.

There was, however, one thing missing — a key to open Pie O'Sky's door. Rupert closed his eyes and sang some of the silly words he had heard standing beside the grand bagoon.

Do you want to roam the sky/like a flying pumpkin pie? He had never even tasted a pumpkin pie much less seen a flying one. He had tasted a *brickberry* pie once and recalled it tasted like moldy dirt rags.

It *had* been a rather large pie, and Rupert figured if it had been bigger he could have sat atop it. But what could possibly make it fly?

It could be picked up by a bunch of strong folks and thrown into the air. Maybe a really strong wind could pick it up.

Watching the Great Bagoon drift down from the sky, he had wondered what his world looked like from so far up. Dashing around the clouds in a flying pumpkin pie would be fun! He could see himself cruising at rooftop level down Fairly Straight Road where Mrs. Drumpsitter lived and scaring the gray out of her hair.

Hmmm, he thought, *I can see myself cruising at rooftop level...*

It was odd, but for a flash of a second he had actually seen in his mind what Fairly Straight Road looked like from high in the air.

How could that be? He had never climbed a phone pole and peered across that street. He had never once stepped onto any of the gray rooftops on Fairly Straight Road and enjoyed the view. And Rupert Dullz was positive he had never taken a seat behind the wheel of a giant flying pumpkin pie and zoomed around Graysland.

So, where had that picture in his mind come from?

If he could see in his mind a place he had never been, then maybe he could also see in his mind a key he had never held. What sort of key could open a door like Pie O'Sky's?

Most of the keys he had seen were made of a silvery metal and pretty much shaped in a typical key shape. He wondered if maybe a key to a place like Far-Myst would have some of the peculiar shades he had seen on Pie O'Sky's bagoon.

What of its shape? It seemed to him likely that nothing in Far-Myst was like anything in Graysland. Would be shaped like a pumpkin? Or a frog? Or maybe a fish?

Yes! A fish with metal scales that weren't silver but rather that bright, happy color he had seen on the rings Pie O'Sky wore on his fingers.

Who knows? Rupert thought. *Maybe the key has a fish shape and can fly.* It seemed everything in Far-Myst could fly. Maybe the fish-key could talk, too. Maybe it could fly up to the door and ask the lock to please open...

Rupert found himself smiling at such silly notions. Then, he began to wonder why they were silly. Surely, if a key did exist for such an untypical door to such an untypical place it would need to be just as untypical. A key that looked like a metal fish of a strange shade that could fly and talk was, in Rupert's mind, very untypical.

He doubted that annoying Tweekus Borm, even with his dumb trunk of a billion keys, had one like that. He doubted anyone would have a key like the one he'd thought of.

A key that he'd thought of! Had he just used his imagination?

How could that be? I don't even have one.

Rupert opened his eyes and saw that his window was glowing with moonlight. With great excitement, he gathered up his bundle and got out of bed and crept out of his room.

Chapter 3

10,000 Keys Plus One

Polgus Dullz was snoring his head off on the sofa. *This shouldn't be too hard*, Rupert thought.

All he had to do was get past his sleeping father, open the front door, and he would be on his way to the clearing at the end of town and Pie O'Sky's bagoon.

He tiptoed to the door. He could feel a blast of air from each snore blow cross his face. His father's breath smelled like his favorite lunch of splage and stinkcheese.

Just a few more feet.

He carefully stepped over the creaky floorboard his father hadn't had a chance to fix and took hold of the doorknob. This would be the last hurdle.

For years, the hinges on the door had been making a noise that sounded like a lonesome cat in a dark alley. Rupert was pretty sure it would not wake his father, but he had to be careful just the same.

He turned the knob and gently pulled the door open.

Eeeeeaaaaayyyyyyyyyy! the hinges sang.

Rupert cringed and looked toward his father, who mumbled something in his sleep and turned over onto his side. Rupert turned back to the door.

Just a few more inches!

Yyyyyaaaaaaaaaaeeeeeeaaaaaaa! cried the hinges.

Rupert froze, closed his eyes and held his breath. His father was still making bear sounds. Taking a deep breath, he stepped outside.

"Hey, Rupert!" Squeem shouted at the top of his stupid lungs, "you got an extra flash-lamp? I couldn't find mine."

"Shhssshhhh!" snapped Rupert.

Too late.

"Rupert Dullz, you come back in here this instant!" Polgus ordered from inside.

"Thanks a lot, Squeem," Rupert complained. "Could you talk any louder?"

"Where do you think you're going at this hour, young man?"

Rupert turned to his father.

"I was lying in bed, and I remembered there were a bunch of big fat bayberry leaves on the drive. I didn't want poor old Grandma to slip and crack her hip."

"Uh-huh," Polgus muttered. "And perhaps a little stroll to go visit that unnatural bagoon that's making every child's tongue wag when they should be thinking of proper things like raking leaves?"

"Honest—I haven't given that bagoon another thought."

"Rupert Dullz, you get back in your bed this very instant! And you, Mister Bissel, I would suggest you do the same before your parents send you off to school tomorrow without so much as a spoonful of splage!"

"That would suit me fine, Mr. Dullz," Squeem said with a goofy smile.

"Home!"

"But, Dad, I figured out how to open the door!"

Polgus's eyes widened, and his great wide forehead wrinkled angrily. He grabbed Rupert by the arm and yanked him inside. He slammed the door so fast the hinges forgot to squeal.

Rupert heard his father lock his bedroom door on the outside. He plopped down on the edge of his bed and buried his chin in his palms.

"Drats!"

"Never mind the improper mouth, Rupert. You get to sleep," his father ordered from the hallway.

Rupert made a series of funny faces at his father through the door and lay down on his back. He stared at the ceiling and wished he could imagine a key to open his own door.

The Grand Bagoon of Pie O'Sky sat in the same clearing where it had landed two days before. The entire field was bathed in the bright gray light of the full moon overhead. A bunch of kids milled about, whispering to each other or showing their methods for opening the door to Far-Myst, which stood once again a few feet from the bagoon.

Pie O'Sky raised his arms high in the air, and the colorful frills on his clothes came to life in the breeze.

"Welcome, children of Graysland! I see we have some brave souls who have returned with the fruits of their imaginations."

"Not me," Tweekus Borm announced as he struggled not to drop a big wooden box he held in both arms. He was dressed in a long black robe and white feetie pajamas. He wore a gray sleeping cap on his head and had a scarf wrapped around his mouth that muffled his words when he spoke.

"I have a box of more than a zillion hundred keys. This stupid door should be a cinch!"

"A zillion hundred?" Pie O'Sky repeated with a wide-eyed grin. "It only takes one to open the door to Far-Myst."

"And I have the one! Somewhere in this box," Tweekus said.

"Then I would suggest you dig through the zillion hundred keys and come up with the correct one," Pie O'Sky suggested.

"But what if I pick the wrong one?" Tweekus now had a worried frown.

"Impossible! If, indeed, you have the correct key, you will surely pick it, and it will open this door. If not, you could pick a key out of your nose, and it would not work."

There were a few chuckles, mostly at Tweekus's expense.

"But…" Tweekus didn't know what to do.

"But, *buttons*! If you have the imagination it takes to get into Far-Myst, it would be utterly impossible for you to pick the wrong key."

"You really think so?"

"Of course!"

Tweekus opened the box and stared at its contents for a moment then plunged his hand into the mass of keys. The other children gathered around. Squeem peered over his shoulder.

"Get back, Squeem, you're in my light," Tweekus ordered. "And where's your dumb friend Rupert?"

"His father caught him trying to sneak out. My big mouth," moaned Squeem.

"Your mouth is bigger than that bagoon," said Tweekus as he fished around in the keys for the one that seemed right.

There was a long pause while only the *tikie-tikie-tinkle* sound of keys filled the cool night air.

Finally, Tweekus drew from the box a single key. It was a large one with a triangle-shaped end. It was shiny gray in color, and tied to it was a tattered strand of white string.

He studied the key and put his face close to the lock on the door. He turned and shot a very cocky smile at Pie O'Sky.

"May I assume by that smile, Mr. Tweekus, that you have made a decision?" Pie O'Sky guessed.

Tweekus was too full of himself to say a word. The ends of his Cheshire cat smile peeked out above the scarf, and he nodded. Pie O'Sky gestured for him to give the key a try. Tweekus started to put the key in the lock but turned suddenly to face Pie O'Sky.

"What happens if it doesn't work?"

"Then you will be on your way home."

Tweekus turned back to the door. All eyes were on him and his silver key. He took a deep breath and inserted it into the lock.

He tried to turn it. He tried again. Mumbles and maybe even a bad word or two sounded from under his scarf. There were some chuckles. Tweekus tried to turn the key a third time without any better luck.

"Frumblestumpaclooparsnot!" mumbled Tweekus. He slapped the door with his palm.

In a sudden flash of brilliant light, he was lifted up into the air. Higher and farther he flew, into the chilly night and back towards the center of Graysland.

There were a few gasps.

"Well, that boy wasn't very imaginative!" Pie O'Sky said. "So, who is next?"

Yukal and Rukal, the twins, stepped up. They held a large hunk of wood in their arms. It was a section of an old telephone pole, and they held it by the steel pegs that workmen used to climb to the top when it was time to fix a busted line or rescue a cat.

"Well, that's a big and strange key!" Pie O'Sky said.

"It ain't no stupid key!" Yukal shouted.

"Then, what does that wooden pole do?"

"Busts stuff open!" Rukal screamed. "*Charge!*"

The two boys aimed the pole and ran full speed toward the door. Pie O'Sky watched with great amusement, and the other kids stared with mouths agape. The pole slammed into the door…

…and in a great flash of light, Yukal and Rukal were launched into the air and, like a pair of ducks, flew up and across the moon and vanished from sight.

There was not a scratch on the door.

"Next!" Pie O'Sky cried like a carnival barker.

Vena Krug stepped up. She looked at Pie O'Sky then back at the remaining four children. Her foehead wrinkled and tightened as she stormed toward the door. She stopped and threw her hands onto her hips.

"Listen, you stupid door! You better open for me, or I'll send you to bed without any splage or sugar soup! And don't give me that snarky sneer! Don't make me mad, or I'll wallop you good!"

Pie O'Sky rolled his eyes and winked. A flash of light exploded, and Vena found herself flying back to her home at a very rapid rate of speed.

"Wow," Squeem mumbled to himself.

Pie O'Sky studied the two remaining children. Squeem did not seem very anxious to step forward. The other, Ubi Ubarky, locked gazes with the bearded man. The boy, a short, skinny kid with a devilish smirk, took from his coat pocket a red stick the size and shape of an empty paper towel tube.

"Another peculiar key," Pie O'Sky said.

"Key, my butt! This is a stick of boomomite. My dad is a street digger. This'll blow any fool door to any crummy place right open!"

"Well, my good lad, why don't you give it a try?"

Ubi raced to the door and laid the stick of boomomite in front of it. He took a single wooden match that was stuck behind his ear and struck it on the doorframe. With his eyes as wide as an owl's, he touched the flame to the fuse, and it flared in a shower of sizzling sparks.

Ubi ran for his life, hiding behind Pie O'Sky, who stood with his arms folded and a funny smirk peeking from his beard. Squeem squinted his eyes and stuck his fingers in his ears. They watched as the fuse burned and burned.

Finally, the fuse stopped burning...and nothing happened. Not a *boom!* Not a *pop!* Not a *pow-a-baddabam!*

"Dribbledrats!" Ubi cried out. "A dud!"

He marched to the door and kicked the stick of boomomite. There was a flash—no sound, just a brilliant flash of light—and like the others, Ubi Ubarky found himself high over Graysland, his bedroom window moving closer and closer until he landed with a firm but painless *plop* atop his mattress.

"So, six minus one minus two minus one times two equals *you* my friend!" Pie O'Sky sang as he examined Squeem with a curious gaze. "What magical mystery imagination station are you going to drive me to?"

"Huh?" Squeem didn't have a clue what Pie O'Sky was talking about.

"The door? Do you have a more clever way to open the door to Far-Myst?"

"No. I don't have a clue. My friend Rupert had a way. Least, that's what he told me. But his father wouldn't let him come here tonight."

"What a shame."

Squeem watched as Pie O'Sky picked up the door and headed back to the basket of his bagoon.

"Wait, Mr. Pie O'Sky! Maybe you could fly over Rupert's house? Maybe he'll see you and run out. Maybe he has a way to open the door."

Pie O'Sky smiled at the thoughtful boy and nodded.

"Maybe, indeed. Maybe, indeed! Where does this young Rupert live?"

"The Curving Road. Seventeen The Curving Road."

There was no way Rupert was going to fall asleep. He lay on his back, his hands clasped behind his head, trying to ignore the hacking and coughing going on next door.

Moonlight still poured through his little round window. It made him sad. The moonlight reminded him of Pie O'Sky and his Grand Bagoon and special doors to special lands. For the rest of his life, Rupert thought, he would be sad every time he saw the moon and was reminded of the chance he'd had to go to a place where anything was possible. A place that might have had the cure for his grandmother's coffus.

He wished the moon would just disappear.

Rupert closed his eyes and wished he would never see moonlight again.

And would you believe it? At that very moment, the bright moonlight falling in through his tiny window vanished. His room went pitch black. Rupert jumped up. There had been no reports of clouds or rain or snow or anything in the sky other than the stars, the moon and the dark night.

He pressed his face against the window. If there had been a contest as to what opened wider — Rupert's eyes or his smile — it would have been a dead tie.

"Pie O'Sky!"

Sure as soap, the Grand Bagoon of Pie O'Sky drifted across the world, its great form blocking out the moon as it passed. It slowly lowered to the street, floating just a few feet above the ground. Rupert's eyes never left the craft.

"Rupert!" came a loud whisper from a face pressed against the other side of the window. Rupert almost jumped out of his skin.

"Squeem!" he whispered back. "What are you doing?"

"Pie O'Sky is here. He wants to see your idea to open the door. Hurry!"

"I'm locked in!"

"So, come out the window!"

Rupert opened the window and climbed into the opening. It was tight. Very tight. In fact, as embarrassed as he was to admit it, he was stuck.

"Hurry!" Squeem repeated.

"I'm stuck. Give me a hand."

Squeem grabbed Rupert's arms and pulled. Little by little, he wormed his way through the tiny opening. He looked at the bagoon. It was drifting down The Curving Road.

"He's leaving! Pie O'Sky's leaving!"

Rupert's words were squeezed out of his body like toothpaste. Squeem pulled with all his might, and finally, with a big tug, Rupert slipped out onto the front yard. He and Squeem toppled over each other, ending up in a pile of leaves and sod.

Rupert jumped to his feet and raced off towards the bagoon.

"Pie O'Sky! Wait! Please wait!"

The bagoon was beginning to lift higher and higher.

"Wait! Don't go!" Rupert screamed. He no longer cared who heard. He didn't care if his parents were awakened and ran out to stop him. This was his last chance. "Pie O'Sky! Come back! I have the key!"

The bagoon rose up, up and away. By the time Rupert dropped his head sadly, it was a mere dot in the sky. He turned to Squeem.

"It's gone. The bagoon is gone."

"So, who needs some old bagoon?"

Rupert turned. It was Pie O'Sky! He stood just off the road beside the special door.

"But you…"

"*But* I am here, young Rupert. The door awaits your key. Tell me, Rupert Dullz, how would you open the door to Far-Myst? Have you used your Imaginings?"

"Imaginings?" Rupert asked, not sure about this new word that sounded very exciting.

"In Far-Myst, the children have an ability we call Imagining. They are able to bring forth, into the real world, things their minds have concocted. Can you as well?"

Rupert took a deep breath and stepped closer to the odd and funny bearded man. He held out his fist and, very slowly, opened it to reveal an empty palm.

"I only see an empty palm," Pie O'Sky said softly.

"It's a key. The key to open the door to Far-Myst," Rupert said with great confidence.

"Can you describe the key to me, Rupert?"

"Yes. It's the same color as those rings you wear."

"You mean gold?" Pie O'Sky asked.

"Yes. Gold. And it's shaped like a fish. It can fly and talk and open that door. It's the most beautiful key ever."

A sugar-filled smiled formed on Pie O'Sky's face. He reached out and took the invisible key from Rupert's hand. Without warning, a fish-shaped key that shimmered and sparkled in the moonlight appeared in his hand

"It is, indeed, the most beautiful key, Rupert," Pie O'Sky said, handing it back. Rupert could only gawk in wonder at the object on his palm.

"Why don't you try it?" Pie O'Sky suggested.

Rupert smiled and spoke to the key.

"Please open the door."

"Yes, Rupert," came the confident voice of the shimmering fish-key.

It floated up and swam through the air to the lock. Then, the fish-key entered the keyhole, turned and dissolved away into a flash of glittering confetti.

The door opened.

Rupert's eyes exploded wider.

"It worked! Squeem, it worked!"

Pie O'Sky stepped forward and placed his hand on Rupert's shoulder.

"Rupert Dullz, you have used your Imaginings well."

"My name is Rupert Starbright. That's the name I want to use," Rupert said proudly as Squeem raised his eyebrows in disbelief.

"If you dare and if you might, enter, Rupert Starbright."

Pie O'Sky took Rupert by the hand and led him to the open door. Rupert's eyes widened as incredible light poured from the portal. He took a look back at his gray world. He shared a smile with Squeem and after three steps was as far from Graysland as he had ever been.

Chapter 4

Not in Graysland Anymore

Rupert's stomach filled with air. The air formed into a tight ball and crawled up his chest into his throat and plopped onto his tongue. Rupert opened his mouth, and one word blasted out like a gigantic belch.

"*Wow!*"

Somehow and impossibly, Rupert was with Pie O'Sky aboard the bagoon and drifting high, high in a sky so blue he was lost in its color. It took a nudge from Pie O'Sky to get him to look down. When he did, he *wowed* again. Brilliantly green rolling hills wandered off to the horizon.

Rupert gripped the edge of the basket and peeked over the side. His eyes were going to pop from their sockets! The grassy hills appeared to be moving like a churning ocean of green water.

"The ground is moving!"

"Those are the Rolling Hills of West Far-Myst."

"How do you walk on it?"

"You don't," Pie O'Sky said with a shrug. "You just sit on your tush and take the ride. Later in the day, the hilliphants come out to graze and ride on those hills."

Rupert's gaze drifted, and his smile doubled. A forest of colors—so many colors and shades of colors—spread out before him. His eyes hurt from the spectacle.

Pie O'Sky pointed one trinket-covered finger.

"And there is Everstood Castle!"

A castle with towers and spires and other things Rupert had never seen before stood like a painting against the bright blue sky.

"That is where the Queen of Far-Myst lives. Queen Chroma. You will be her special guest."

A sudden gust of wind tossed Rupert's hair, and he shivered in the chill. He threw his arms around his chest and blew into his clenched hands.

"There is a chill coming from the south," Pie O'Sky said softly.

Rupert glanced to his right and frowned.

"*That* isn't very colorful," he said with a nervous shiver.

A band of black clouds that oozed and dripped like tar hovered across the southern sky. Pie O'Sky forced a tiny smile, but his eyes were filled with concern.

"It's getting closer," the purple-bearded man whispered.

"What is?"

Pie O'Sky pushed a bigger smile onto his face and pointed west.

"The castle! Everstood Castle! We'll be landing soon."

Rupert turned his attention back to the castle, but another wicked gust sent another chill up his back. Pie O'Sky shivered as well.

As the bagoon sank, Rupert could see that Far-Myst was even more beautiful close up. He stared with wide-eyed wonder as the bagoon floated over lush and well-kept gardens and town squares. Everstood Castle was like nothing he had ever laid eyes on. The stones that formed the mighty walls were speckled with shimmering colors, as if trillions of tiny jewels were embedded in them. In the glow of the sun, the castle seemed to dance in a mighty rainbow of fire.

Pie O'Sky placed two fingers in his mouth and let out an eardrum-popping whistle that seemed to echo across the land forever. He whistled three more times.

"What are you doing?" Rupert asked, rubbing an ear with his finger.

"Calling a hole. They're usually grazing up on the foothills of the lower Feign Mountains around this time. Keep your eyes open on the eastern horizon."

Rupert had no clue what he was looking for, but he shielded his eyes from the bright sun and peered out to the east.

"Look, Rupert, here comes one," Pie O'Sky shouted.

Sure enough, flapping across the sky and approaching at great speed was a black disk larger than the bagoon. It came gently to rest on a large field of grass within the walls of Everstood Castle.

To Rupert's surprise and delight, a hole—a large and deep one—now awaited them.

"A hole!" He pointed with delight.

Pie O'Sky gave him an odd look softened by a smile.

"Isn't that what I just said? The holes nibble on the sweet grasses and bitter roots of the hills. What do holes eat where you come from?"

"They kinda just sit in the street until somebody comes along and fills them up."

"You mean you *kill* holes in Graysland?" Pie O'Sky sounded shocked.

"I guess. I never really though much about them. Where I live, holes are just stupid things people fall into and crack their hips."

"Everything in Far-Myst is alive. That's why everything in Far-Myst is interesting. Now, hold on, Rupert Starbright. Down we go."

The bagoon lowered down, down, down. Rupert was surprised to discover that the inside of the hole was not the darkened cave he had expected. As they descended deeper and deeper, the walls became more and more fanciful—adorned with great paintings displaying important moments in Far-Myst history.

A wide lake of glowing blue water sat at the bottom of the hole, and in it was an island. A flat landing area with a giant letter X glowing across its surface awaited them.

Pie O'Sky brought the bagoon down past huge, colorful stalactites and stalagmites. They reminded Rupert of the icicles that often formed on the edge of his roof, only these were the size of tall buildings and no two were the same color.

He was also certain he spotted pairs of large eyes staring at him from each of the rocky formations.

The bagoon landed perfectly in the center of the X. Pie O'Sky opened the door on the basket and gestured for Rupert to follow him.

"Welcome to Everstood Castle. Well, the deep dungeon, at least. Queen Chroma lives in the castle proper — ten levels up. We will take the chairmen."

Pie O'Sky whistled again, this time with softer and more melodic tones.

On the shore of the lake that surrounded the landing island appeared two large chairs. They ran on their four legs like gazelles and crossed the water on a narrow bridge, coming to a stop when they reached Rupert and Pie O'Sky.

"Welcome, Pie O'Sky. I would be honored to carry you wherever you wish to go," said the first chairman, who was upholstered in red felt. The other chairman was covered in deep-purple silk.

"A child?" the purple chairman said. "I have not seen one in ages. May I transport you, my young master?"

Rupert looked up to Pie O'Sky, unsure how to respond.

"You can take us both to the Queen's Chamber of Music," Pie O'Sky requested.

"Hop on!" offered the red chairman.

"Yes! Hop on, indeed!" the purple chairman said to Rupert with a bow.

Rupert and Pie O'Sky took seats, and the chairmen galloped back across the bridge.

Rupert's heart raced with every bound and leap his chairman took along the twisting, colorful halls and passageways of Everstood Castle. It was eleven lifetimes of sights, sounds and smells as he raced up the wide, gently rising spiral staircases. He passed great windows at each landing that showed ever grander views of Far-Myst.

Finally, like in the final stretch of a horse race, the two chairmen galloped side-by-side down a long corridor and finally stopped before a crystal door.

"Ha. Beat ya by a trump," the red chairmen bragged, lifting one of his claw-footed legs.

"Ah, sit on yourself!" the purple chair snapped. "Here you go, my good fellow. The Queen's Chamber of Music."

Pie O'Sky and Rupert stood up and thanked the chairmen, who raced back down the hallway, vanishing as quickly as they had arrived.

Rupert studied the marvelous crystal doors, which were decorated with all sorts of exotic musical instruments. Soft and beautiful sounds drifted from beyond them. Pie O'Sky smiled, stepped up to the door and touched the inlaid image of a golden flute. A pretty series of music notes played. The doors opened.

"Follow me, Starbright. Time to meet the queen."

Rupert had never met a queen. As a matter of fact, he wasn't even sure if he knew what a queen was. He was pretty sure she was an important person who was in charge of things, sort of like the principal of his school back in Graysland. He hoped Queen Chroma was not the old grumpy pest Mrs. Chickbump was.

When he looked up and found himself staring into two bright grass-green eyes and a warm, sincere smile, all those worries vanished.

"Queen Chroma," Pie O'Sky said with a bow, "may I present to you Rupert Starbright."

Rupert stepped forward and nodded nervously. He found it hard to look at Queen Chroma, yet he also found it hard *not* to look at her.

Her face was bright and cat-like, and her eyes were the same color as the grass of the Rolling Hills. She had hair braided in two long twists that fell one over each shoulder. Although it was black, it shimmered, like the stones of the castle, with every color of the rainbow. She wore a simple, medium-length gown of a material that looked like pearls.

The room was decorated with a rich royal-purple carpet and tile walls of soft cream and raspberry. A window opened onto the expanse of Far-Myst's Northern Region. It was a spectacular view.

But perhaps the most amazing thing in the room was the source of the music. Floating in the air were a dozen shiny brass, woodwind and stringed instruments. They played themselves and danced in the air to the beat of their own tune.

Rupert's eyes felt like ping-pong balls, bouncing among the unfamiliar and very un-ordinary sights.

"I am very glad to meet you, Rupert Starbright," Queen Chroma said with great warmth. "Did you enjoy the chairman ride?"

"Yes. The chairs in Graysland just sit around like chairs."

The queen smiled. "Would you like a more lei-surely tour of the castle and its grounds?"

"That would be great."

"I look forward to seeing a sample of your powerful Imaginings."

Rupert seemed quite puzzled.

"I just want to find a way to cure my grand-mother of the coffus."

"The coffus?" the queen wondered.

"She coughs all the time. My father says the cof-fus brings the coffin."

"Well, that won't do," said Queen Chroma sympathetically. "I am sure, Rupert, you will be able to imagine a cure."

"I sure hope so."

"Rupert has shown much potential," Pie O'Sky explained.

Her eyebrow suddenly rose, and she looked at him curiously.

"Looks like the ride on the chairman drained the color from your beard, Pie O," she said.

He turned to the crystal door and peeked at his reflection. Sure enough, his purple beard was pur-ple no more.

"She's right—your beard is gray!" Rupert waved his finger wildly.

Pie O'Sky continued to study his reflection. His forehead wrinkled more as he noticed large blotches of gray had appeared on his clothing and hat.

"The purple in my clothes is gone, too." The perplexed glaze that filled his eyes quickly changed to panic. He shot a glance at Queen Chroma. She was staring at the carpet.

Rupert looked down, and his mouth fell open. It, too, was now a bland gray.

"The carpet! Its color ran away," he shouted.

"The Pigments?" Pie O'Sky wondered aloud.

The queen's eyes now shared the same panic.

"To the Pigment pens!" she ordered as she raced from the room.

Chapter 5

Pigs Have Flown

Rupert followed Pie O'Sky and the queen down a flight of winding stairs and a very, very long hallway. The hall was lined with stained glass windows and tall potted plants with strange fruit and flowers in vivid colors.

Along the way, a number of the Royal Guards joined the race, pleading with the queen to let them handle the situation. She would have none of that, so the guards surrendered the lead to her and followed close behind.

Rupert studied the queen as they ran. She was definitely not, as Rupert's father would say, *somebody who made other people rake her leaves*. Mrs. Drumpsitter wouldn't even clean her own blackboard—Squeem had to wipe it to a sparkling shine with a dripping wet sponge every morning.

They ran across a small footbridge and through a number of towers until finally they emerged in a town square. Rupert's gaze darted from side to side as he zipped past vendors selling fruit and flowers and small shops that displayed clothing, musical instruments, farm tools and huge slabs of meats and cheeses.

His attention was drawn to a small brick structure with a sign that read: EVERSTOOD SCHOOL OF MINDMATTER PRACTICES. The building appeared to be empty, and its doors were closed. No lights burned in the windows.

There were many people milling about, making purchases and discussing local gossip. When they spotted Queen Chroma, a half-dozen castle guards, Pie O'Sky and a small boy, the tongues really began wagging. They took special interest in Rupert.

"A child!" murmured a fat woman with an armful of bread.

"Where did he come from?" said an old man struggling with a sack of potatoes.

"Do you suppose he was brought back?" a man with six colorful parrots on his shoulders wondered.

"A child! It's a child!" screeched one of the parrots.

"Is that possible?" wondered a tall fellow selling handmade jewelry.

The queen finally came to a stop near a golden building in the center of the square. The door was open. She entered, and the guards quickly followed. Rupert stopped Pie O'Sky with a tug on his sleeve.

"Where are all the children?" he asked.

Pie O'Sky's face went through some very serious expressions until it relaxed into his usual smile.

"We'll explain it all to you. First, come see the Seven Pigments."

They stepped into the shade of the building, which Rupert soon discovered smelled very mucky. It was a barn made of bright cherry wood with a large, tinted skylight that cooled the sunlight as it poured in from above.

The queen and two of the guards were at the far end talking to a stocky man in dirty clothing and muddy boots. He had a full head of silver hair, and even from the distance, Rupert could see the man's intense, serious eyes. They all stood staring into the last of a row of large pens.

"This, Rupert, is where the Seven Pigments live."

Pie O'Sky took a few of his long strides to the first pen. Sitting inside on a comfy bed of hay and mud was a huge, apple-red pig.

"This first one is named Red."

"It's a pig," Rupert deduced.

"No, it's a Pigment. All the colors in Far-Myst are made possible by these seven Pigments. We have cared for and honored them since the beginning of time. The Pigments are the source of the wondrous hues that color this great land." Pie O'Sky continued on past the next pens. "He is Orange, and she Yellow."

Rupert was amazed at both the size and brilliant colors of the amazing porkers. He was shown the next three Pigments—Green, Blue and Indigo. Finally, they stopped beside the queen and the muddy-booted man and understood what all the fuss was about.

The last pen was empty.

"Violet's gone?" Pie O'Sky gasped.

The queen nodded somberly.

"Yes, I'm afraid so. Nightwingers."

"That slime Murkus is getting bolder," said the man with the muddy boots, speaking the name *Murkus* like a terrible curse.

"Who is Murkus?" Rupert asked.

"Not a nice fellow," was Pie O'Sky's brief answer.

"Who is this boy, Your Highness?" the man asked as he studied Rupert with both curiosity and distrust.

"I've been rude to our guest. Dream Weaver, this is young Rupert Starbright. He comes from a land far away. Rupert, this is Dream Weaver, the greatest gardener in all of Far-Myst."

Rupert shyly shook the hand of Dream Weaver. The man's hand felt very powerful, and the man's intense eyes startled him.

"Welcome," the gardener grunted." I would suggest you go back to the safety of your homeland."

"But I thought Far-Myst was a place of imagination and good stuff?"

"Weaver," Pie O'Sky said, "Rupert may be of great help. He is a boy of potentially strong Imaginings."

Dream Weaver shook his head doubtfully and gave Pie O'Sky a funny look.

Rupert's mind had been filling with so many questions since his arrival he could contain them no more. He felt he was being kept in the dark about something — something very important.

He threw his hands to his hips and looked Pie O'Sky hard in the eyes.

"What is going on here? What are nightwingers? Who is Murkus? How come there aren't any kids around? Why did the purple pig disappear and your beard turn gray? How about that ugly-looking storm?"

Dream Weaver smiled at the boy's tenacity. Queen Chroma and Pie O'Sky both gave Rupert a silent, heartfelt gaze.

"You are right, Rupert," Pie O'Sky confessed sadly. "Far-Myst is in a bad way. We need your help."

"*My* help? You all have so much imagination! I don't have any. What good can I do?"

"Your Imagining abilities created the most clever key. It was the most colorful and the most imaginative I have ever seen. But more important than that, Rupert, the only reason you wanted to come here was to help your grandmother get well."

"So, what's wrong with that?"

"Nothing is wrong with that, Rupert," Queen Chroma told him. "It is wonderfully right. Pie O'Sky has searched many, many lands for just the right child. Most wanted to come here for selfish reasons. I can see why he chose you."

"The right child for what?"

"To Imagine a way to stop the darkness that has entered Far-Myst. A darkness that has robbed us of our children. A darkness that is attempting to steal from Far-Myst its very heart—its imagination."

"Why can't you or Pie O'Sky or Mr. Weaver Imagine the answer?"

"In this land, Rupert, only the children have the full power to wield the Imagining. A power that fades greatly with age. Adults can imagine great tales and compose music and create art, but only the children can use the Imagining. Only a child can actually bring into reality the objects of their imaginations," Pie O'Sky said.

Rupert grew sad, and his gaze fell to his own shoes. He kicked a small stone.

"So, you tricked me. You tricked me to come here so I can help you."

"It looks that way," mumbled Weaver, giving Pie O'Sky a dirty look.

"The only thing sadder than a child without imagination is imagination without a child," replied Pie O'Sky, offering Dream Weaver a gentle smile. The gardener looked away.

"All I did was imagine a flying fish key."

"That was very big for a boy who thought he had no imagination," Pie O'Sky told him.

"And it was just the beginning," said Queen Chroma, putting a gentle hand on Rupert's shoulder. "You will discover, with the help of great teachers at the Everstood School of Mindmatter Practices, that you can learn to awaken the full power that sleeps inside you,".

Dream Weaver shook his head and looked away.

"Pie O'Sky, why don't you show Rupert the Child's Eye Museum. Let him see first-hand what a child can do in Far-Myst. Then we will serve him a hearty meal and explain in great detail what's going on."

Rupert's eyes widened with great interest.

Pie O'Sky nodded and walked Rupert out of the Pens as well as the earshot of the Queen and Weaver. Two Castle guards followed.

Chapter 6

Danger from Above!

"Weaver? What's wrong?" the queen asked.

Dream Weaver replied softly, "With all due respect, Your Highness, do you really think we should be putting this boy in such danger? To have tricked him the way you did?"

Queen Chroma nodded. "You may be right, Weaver. But what choice do we have? We need a child. The situation is growing more desperate. Have you seen the storm? The entire southern sky is black. Black with Murkus's influence. We can keep Rupert safe. We will never let him out of our sight."

Dream Weaver sighed hard and nodded in turn.

"I'm just a simple gardener, but I can only think of my own young Quix and Fancy. I do not want to see another child vanish. I know how much it hurts."

Queen Chroma gently lifted his downcast chin with one hand.

"You are a loyal and trusted friend. We will defeat Murkus. And when we do, you will be reunited with Quix and Fancy. As will all the parents and children of Far-Myst."

"Yes. Yes, we will, Your Highness."

"In the meantime, I am leaving it up to you to keep Rupert safe."

"*Me?*"

"You. Until we can train him properly."

Weaver looked away a moment then turned to the queen and nodded.

All adult eyes were on Rupert as Pie O'Sky led him through the square towards the oddly shaped structure at the end of the main road. Sprinkled in with the whispers were questions, shouted out to the boy.

"Have you seen my little girl, Fuschia?"

"Is Murkus treating the children well?"

"I hear you can climb rainbows and turn mountains into ice cream!"

"Will you help us get our children back?"

"I will be happy to adopt you if you cannot find your parents."

Rupert's eyes shot from person to person. The sad voices asking the questions choked him up, and he was unable to answer any of them. Pie O'Sky and the two guards did their best to shield him, but the crowd was desperate for answers.

"Where were all of their kids taken?" he asked.

"I wish we knew, Rupert." Pie O'Sky sighed.

They climbed the winding steps to the strange building that housed the Child's Eye Museum. It floated more than fifty feet above the ground like a giant cloud but was shaped like a many-pointed star. All of the walls were made of thick, colorful glass that allowed a tiny peek inside.

They stepped through the main doors, and Rupert's eyes again grew wide at sight of more of the wonders of Far-Myst.

"What is all this stuff?" He couldn't even guess.

"These, Rupert Starbright, are just a small sample of the things a child's Imaginings can create."

There were so many objects of so many shapes, sizes and colors it made Rupert dizzy. The objects were either enclosed in clear glass cases or hung in mid-air by something invisible.

There was a thing that looked like a giant starfish that blew soap bubbles that popped to form a snowfall of gumdrops.

A giant umbrella spun like a top and sprayed showers of multicolored sparks that made music notes, creating a continuous, ever-changing song.

A rubber ball with seventeen eyes danced a silly dance while juggling giggling apples and oranges with its fifteen hands.

A flock of colorful kites soared through the air, creating glowing rainbows that were transformed into clothing by a pair of giant lobster tailors.

Across the room, hovering in the air, was a large round mirror with a golden frame. A never-ending line of strange birds, fish, fruit and flowers came out from the surface of the mirror, and each turned into a large colorful word that formed the sentences and pages of an exciting storybook. A voice spoke from a toothy mouth on the mirror's frame, reading the story aloud.

"Kids made all this?"

"With their Imagining abilities, yes. Many of these items were discovered lying about in the nearby forest."

"Why in the forest?"

"Quite often, a child will lie in bed at night and dream up these magical things. Sometimes, when their skills have not been perfected, the things they Imagine will appear, but not where the child meant them to."

"Far-Myst seems like a happy place to live, if it didn't have such unhappy problems."

"You are very right, Rupert Starbright. But happy times will come again."

"Graysland is so boring. My school is boring. The other kids are boring. All those stupid dead leaves and rakes are really, really boring."

Pie O'Sky placed his hand on Rupert's shoulder and smiled. His smile didn't last, though, as a swarm of shadows crossed outside the glassy walls and ceiling of the museum.

A guard cried out, "Wingers!"

The muffled sound of screams came from outside, and horrible screeches cracked the air. There was a tremendous crash and the sound of shattering glass.

Pie O'Sky grabbed Rupert by the arm and pulled him to safety under the wide arch of the doorway. Glass fell like deadly hail all around them. When the fall of glass ended, Rupert peeked out and gasped at the creatures entering through the hole in the roof.

They looked like giant cockroach men. Their heads were bony and had two long antennas that flapped behind them as they flew on thick, leathery wings. The bodies of the invaders, though, were more like a man's than an insect's. Strong and muscular, their skin was like black armor.

They gave out terrible squeals and screeches as they flew, their red eyes scanning for targets.

"Come, Rupert, we must get back to the castle!" Pie O'Sky yanked the boy out of the museum. The two guards followed closely.

There was chaos in the town square. People ran for cover as dozens of nightwingers swooped out of the sky. Squads of guards had appeared, and many were surrounding the Golden Pen to protect the remaining Six Pigments. They fought the flying monsters with swords and poles and bare hands.

Pie O'Sky kept Rupert close with one arm around his shoulder as he ducked and searched for the clearest path back to the castle.

"Why are they attacking?" Rupert asked.

"These are the beasts of Murkus. They do his dirty work," Pie O'Sky explained as he pushed through the frantic crowd. "Murkus wants nothing less than the complete destruction of Far-Myst's imagination. He wants his dark cloud to cover all the world."

"Get that boy to safety immediately!" Queen Chroma ordered over the roar of the turmoil.

Rupert turned and was surprised to see the queen fighting side-by-side with the guards. She used a dagger that sent out colorful waves of rainbow light. The colors drove away the nightwingers, who fled in terror.

52

Rupert smiled, just for a second, as he tried to picture what Mrs. Drumpsitter would do in such a situation. *Probably bore them to sleep with stuff about leaf bags and file cabinets.*

His thoughts were interrupted by a sharp tug. He turned, and his face went snow-white. He watched stunned as Pie O'Sky, grabbed by two nightwingers, was carried higher and higher into the air.

"Pie O'Sky!"

It was too late. Pie O'Sky was no more than a colorful smudge.

Rupert suddenly felt very much alone, and for the first time since coming through the door, he was scared. A dark shadow crossed over him. A nightwinger reached for him. The air that blew on his face from the terrible beating wings smelled like the dead mouse he had found under a leaf bag once. Only it was a hundred times stronger.

He threw himself to the ground, and the horrid critter flew past. Many people were running by him; screams and shouts and curses of disgust filled the air. He searched among the crowd of bodies for a clear path.

Catching a glimpse of daylight he jumped to his feet. He could see the entrance to the castle just a few yards away. He took off in a dash.

"Almost there," he whispered, growing out of breath.

Something touched his shoulder. It was an ice-cold grip. The wind of batting wings blew back his hair, and he could smell the stink of a hundred dead mice. He turned to find himself face-to-face with the insect face of a nightwinger.

Rupert screamed as he was picked up off the ground a couple of feet. He swung his fists at the creature. He kicked as hard as he could. It was like fighting a wall—an ugly, stinking, rock-hard wall.

A great shout filled the air. It wasn't the nightwinger, and it wasn't Rupert.

"Drop that boy, you disgusting beast!"

Rupert felt the ground hit his bottom as he was released from the grip of the monster. Dream Weaver stepped between him and the horror. With a swipe of a glowing dagger similar to the queen's, he chased the creature skyward with waves of colorful light.

"Come on, boy. Quickly!"

Dream Weaver lifted Rupert with one arm. He raced through the crowd and made it safely under an overhang of vines with bright-red flowers. He continued down a stony path to the cover of a bunch of giant trees.

The chaos of the town square faded. Rupert felt dizzy. He closed his eyes.

Chapter 7

Murky Muck and Murkus

Murkus sat on a throne of filth—a massive seat made from a nasty collection of animal droppings shaped and formed like sculptor's clay. His private chambers looked like a cave carved out of solid coal. The only light that dared to enter was the soft sunlight that struggled through a single dirty window.

Murkus was a giant of a man. His massive legs were like logs jutting from the wide seat. His large head was hairless—not even eyebrows or eyelashes—and his skin was a sickly yellowish-blue color. His eyes were small and set far apart, and his mouth seemed to smile and frown at the same time—each end of his lips was aimed in a different direction.

He was dressed in chain mail and filthy brown leather that was cracked and worn. His large fists, the size of melons, impatiently pounded the throne's wide arms. His mouth opened to reveal sharp yellow and green teeth as he roared, "Slog! Get in here!"

Down a long, wet corridor came footsteps as Slog splashed through the twisting intestines of Murkus's lair. He was a skinny critter who looked something like a nightwinger, but he lacked the powerful muscles of his kind. His wings were nothing but tattered nubs, as if they had been ripped off his body by angry, powerful hands.

"I'm coming, your masterful leadership," he mumbled. "I shall report good news. No need to hit. No need for fists. Good news. Good news, Lord Murkus!" He peeked around the entrance into the throne room. "Lord Murkus?"

There was a flash of leather and chain mail, and Slog floated through the air — lifted off his feet by a large hand and pulled into the room. He dangled face-to-face with Murkus.

"Good news," Slog chirped meekly.

"You are late, Slog. I am tired of waiting for you. I have things to do."

"Sorry, sire, but the flyers just —"

"What is the news?"

"The news? Oh, yes. The news. We have captured the clown."

"The clown? The flyers have captured Pie O'Sky?"

Slog nodded excitedly.

"You mean that color-loving, tune-whistling, bagoon-flying, imagination-spouting pest is finally in my grasp?"

Slog nodded again.

Murkus dropped him to the floor like a clump of cat litter and laughed victoriously. Slog got back to his feet and danced and clapped his hands, sharing his master's excitement.

"Their defenses were a joke, milord. Only two Illuminors."

"Even the Illuminors will be powerless against me when my shadowlight falls upon Far-Myst," Murkus mumbled to himself.

"That greensman was more concerned with the boy than with defending the castle."

Murkus's look made Slog step back.

"Of course, the boy *is* no concern. Just a powerless tyke. No concern! No concern, milord!"

"A boy?"

"A boy. Just one. A skinny, wimpy-looking lad. He is not even from Far-Myst! Not a threat, definitely not a threat!"

The large hand of Murkus once again clamped around Slog's neck.

"A *child*? There is a *child* from another land? Living in Far-Myst? Why is he not here with the others?"

"As reported, milord, he managed to escape the flyers. Help from the greensman."

Murkus's face contorted into pure hatred as he mouthed the word *greensman*.

"That *gardener* dares to get in the way of my plan?"

"He's that sort of fellow, I suppose," squeaked Slog.

Once again, Slog was dropped like an old rag. Murkus paced and pounded his thighs with his fists.

"I want that boy! They may do what they will to the gardener, but I want the boy alive. There will be no Imaginings in Far-Myst ever again! Bring the brat to me!"

"Yes, yes, yes, milord!"

Slog bowed over and over, backing quickly out of the throne room. He ran through a maze of halls that wound and dipped and climbed, finally opening into a tremendous dining room. Hundreds of nightwingers sat at old, dirty wooden tables gobbling up rotting fruit and spoiled meat.

Slog passed the order to one of the squad leaders of the flyers. *Get the child. Do what you will with the gardener, but bring back the child to Murkus. Alive.*

Murkus slid his beefy hand across the rusty bars of the prison cell. The giant rings on his fingers screeched with a bone-chilling sound.

"Hello, my clown," he greeted Pie O'Sky, flashing his green teeth.

Inside the narrow, damp prison cell, Pie O'Sky was tied-up, blindfolded and bathed in pure darkness projected by the sinister shadowlights.

"Do you like my shadowlights, Clown? Nasty little invention of mine. A tiny sample of what is to come for Far-Myst. A world filled with fear, terror and horrible dreams. Do you feel your mind draining? Do you feel that horrid imagination of yours slipping away? Dissolving into darkness?"

Pie O'Sky turned his face to Murkus and smiled.

"Not yet."

"Oh, it will, colorful friend. It will. Now, tell me, who is the child?"

"The who?"

"I understand a boy has arrived as guest to Queen Chroma. Was saved from my wingers by that plant lover. Who is this child?"

"I think your wingers need to have their eyesight examined. Perhaps they mistook poor Violet for a child."

"That pig will make a delicious breakfast. As will all of them. *Who* is the *child*?"

"You're so clever with your wingers and shadowlights. You tell me," said Pie O'Sky.

Murkus slammed his palm against the bars. The *clang!* bounced around the stone hallways of the keep.

"Tease all you want, Clown, but as that darkness pulls on your mind, you will grow weary. Sad. Horror will seep into your thoughts. Then you will beg me to help capture that young bird."

Murkus stormed off.

Chapter 8

Of Pepper Poets and Juggling Geraniums

"Boy! Boy, wake up," Weaver said, shaking Rupert's shoulder.

Rupert mumbled about dead mice and bat wings and finally opened his eyes, tossing nervous glances about.

"It's okay. We should be safe from them wingers in here," Weaver assured him.

Rupert sat up and found he was on the surface of a gigantic mushroom the size of the sofa back in his living room at home. He took a good look at the odd lump of fungus. It was white with yellow and red spots. A thin pink mist rose from the red-colored polka dots and sent a pleasing smell wafting into his nose. He felt suddenly calm.

"This looks like the little mushrooms that grow under the steps of my house. Only way bigger."

"Not a mushroom," Weaver grunted, rising to his feet and scanning their surroundings. "It's a lushroom. A kind of fungus. Helps calm the nerves and relax the muscles. You got faint from the fright."

Rupert rubbed his temples and took another whiff of the air. He looked at the peculiar lushroom and stroked its surface.

"And treat it with respect. It's over a hundred years old. Its name is Sylus."

Rupert took a deep breath of the spicy mist and made his way to his feet. Sylus adjusted its shape and seemed to help him gently upright.

"So, where are we?"

"The Garden of Dreams."

"Garden? This looks more like a forest. The gardens we have back home are just square plots of grass and dead leaves."

Weaver filled his lungs with the wonderful air and spread his arms proudly.

"These are the wondrous gardens of Far-Myst. I have been the chief gardener for more than twenty years. Every plant, every bush and flower, every fungus and vine and blade of grass is like my own child. Nowhere, Mister Starbright, will you find a greater collection of growing things than you will see here."

"Can you show me all the different plants? Take me on a tour?"

"Your only worry is to stay in sight. I have to figure a way to get you back home."

"But why? I want to see more of Far-Myst. I want to see if I can Imagine a cure for my grandmother's coffus."

"You will do as I say! Can't you see the danger all the folk of Far-Myst are in? Those nightwingers are not butterfloats or singerbirds. They are the filthy servants of Murkus! They're dangerous. Can't you feel the chill in the air?"

Rupert looked at the sky. Through the breaks in the canopy of trees, it was still blue.

"Drats, I thought this was going to be really unboring, but it's just a bunch of super-boring rules and adults telling me to go home."

"You bet your skinny backside! You stay close. You listen to what I tell you, Starbright."

"My real name is Dullz. Rupert Dullz," Rupert snapped back.

"Fine. Dullz it is."

Rupert took another deep breath and exhaled hard. His attention fell suddenly upon a very unboring sight a few yards away. Colorful balls of light were dancing in the air. He raced off to investigate.

"Dullz!" Weaver shouted. "What did I tell you?"

Rupert stopped in front of the octopus-like bush. It had thick branches covered in rich green leaves the shape of hearts. The plant was juggling glowing fruit!

"I can't believe this," Rupert gasped.

Weaver stepped up behind him.

"Did I not just tell you to stay within sight?"

"I never saw a tree like this!"

"It's not a tree. It's a plant. And of course you've never seen one. They only grow in Far-Myst. It's a juglanium. Juggles its fruit to keep them from being eaten by birds and animals and nosy kids."

Purple, yellow, orange and sky-blue fruit floated and arched as more than twenty-five arm-like branches kept them all afloat.

"Squeem and Vena and especially that boring butt Tweekus will never believe this. Can you show me more plants and trees and stuff?"

"No time for tours. We have to set up a camp."

"What about the wingers?"

"They hate this place. Too much of Nature's imagination. Frightens them off. At least, it always has. Buggers have been getting bolder."

"What will happen to Pie O'Sky?"

"I don't know."

"What about the queen? Can she fight them all off herself?"

"She isn't by herself. She has the entire Palace Guard Force. And she has an Illuminor."

"What's an Illuminor?"

"Stop asking so many questions. We have to set up a campsite."

Weaver grabbed Rupert by the hand and pulled him off through the Gardens of Dreams. They walked without rest for a solid half-hour. Rupert could only catch glimpses of the many, many wonders growing all around.

There were flowers with petals that fluttered about like swarms of moths and trees that danced with the music of the birds. Large bushes of firefly berries flashed messages, while carpenter trees grew fully formed tables and chairs that hung like weird fruit from their branches. Carpets of orchestra grass played great musical works as deadly dragon shrubs waited for a passing bird or large insect to come close enough to roast with a fiery blast for a tasty meal.

They walked under an avenue of waterfall pines that sent refreshing mists into the air from the great streams of water that ran down their bark. Sadsack bushes whispered mournful tales, merry mint plants giggled, and bloodybarks frightened all their little saplings with tales of horror.

Finally, Weaver came to a stop in a small clearing beside a pretty pond that was enclosed in a ring of tall trees with immense trunks. Many bushes and tall plants surrounded the clearing.

"We'll set up camp here, near the spectral oaks."

He pointed to the seven giants that surrounded the pond. Each had leaves of one color of the rainbow, like the Pigments—red, orange, yellow, green, blue, indigo and violet.

"I thought that color was gone since the wingers stole Violet," Rupert said, pointing to the handsome oak with rich purple leaves.

"Everything violet or purple will fade as long as Violet is away from Far-Myst. The Violet Oak will sadly be gray by the next sunrise."

Weaver knelt down next to a tiny yellow toadstool that grew beside a small rock. He looked around then nodded as something caught his eye.

"Make yourself useful, Dullz—go pick a leaf from that blue bush with the silver berries. Only one! And do not damage the nightlight moss growing below it."

Rupert nodded and did as he was asked. He carefully plucked one of the long and narrow leaves and returned it to Dream Weaver.

"Watch and learn something, Dullz. The bull-frog stool and the silverberry plant have never been the best of friends. They love to outdo each other, like brothers and sisters. The silverberry attracts the nightlight moss that glows in brilliant colors. Tries to make the bullfrog stool jealous."

"What does the bullfrog stool do?"

"This." Weaver touched the leaf to the little mushroom, and in a flash, it grew to more than fifty times its original size. The result was a large, round, hollow growth that resembled a tent.

"As long as the leaf touches it, the bullfrog stool will remain this size. The inside is hollow and a lot warmer than out here. That'll be your bed."

"Amazing." Rupert shook his head and smiled. "What about you?"

"Never mind about me. I'll sleep under the trees. Out of doors. I like the night air on my brow."

Weaver placed the leaf inside the bullfrog-stool shelter and stepped to the shore of the pond. He stared into the crystal-clear water as if searching for something.

Finally, he plunged his hand under the surface and came up with a large clump of wet, muddy grass. He returned to the clearing and plopped it onto the ground.

"Gather some rocks, about this size," Weaver ordered, holding his hands about six inches apart.

"What for?"

"We are going to eat them for supper," Weaver said with a roll of his eyes. "Never mind what for. Just get them. And be careful where you step."

Rupert pouted and sauntered off. *He's just like my parents and boring teachers. Always ordering us to do boring chores.*

"And stay in sight," Weaver called after him.

"Yes, Mr. Weaver," Rupert moaned.

As he found each stone, he was told to place it in a circle around the mound of wet pond grass. He had gathered six stones and was seeking the final one needed to complete the ring when a soft, high-pitched voice called to him.

"Hey! Hey, human!"

Rupert darted his eyes about, looking for the source of the voice.

"Who said that?"

"I'm right in front of your face. The green plant with the little red peppers. Sheesh. For someone wandering the gardens with the chief gardener you sure are dumb."

"I'm not dumb! It's just that where I come from plants and trees only drop dead leaves. They don't juggle or glow or annoy people."

"You want to see something really, really amazing."

"What?"

"Pick one of my peppers and eat it."

"Mr. Weaver told me not to touch anything."

"Are my peppers growing off Weaver's arms and legs? Pick a pepper and pop it in your big mouth."

Hesitantly, Rupert lifted the tiny brilliant-red fruit to his nose.

"Don't smell it. Just throw it in your mouth. Chew it real good and swallow it."

Rupert did. For a few seconds, he just froze, and his eyes widened. Then his cheeks turned as red as the pepper, and he gasped.

"What are you trying to do, kill me?" he asked, hopping up and down on one foot and waving his hands at his tongue.

The plant was giggling.

"If you can't stand the heat, get out of the garden!" The pepper plant giggled some more.

"Not funny. That was *hot*."

"Yeah, I know. But now comes the fun part. Tell me the story."

"What story?"

"The one I grew. The one you just ate. I grow tons of them. Poems, stories. I hear them in the wind. Or discussed by the trees. I'm a pepper poet plant."

"A what?" Rupert asked, still waving his hand before his open mouth.

"A pepper poet plant. A tongue-twister, I'll admit. I stick the stories in the peppers and wait for some sucker like you to come along, eat them and recite to me my literary brilliance. I'm the hottest author in these gardens."

The plant laughed again, and Rupert rolled his eyes.

"Get it? *Hottest* author! I crack myself up!"

"You're sneaky."

"I know. So, tell me my story."

"I don't know what you are talking..." Rupert stopped speaking as a smile filled his face. "That's weird."

"What is, kid?"

"I hear words in my head. They're just popping in."

"What the heck did I just finish telling you? Tell me my story."

"*Your* story? It's *my* story! The words are about me and Pie O'Sky coming to Far-Myst in his ba-goon."

"Mister Dullz! Are you done with the fire ring yet?" Weaver shouted.

"Just getting the last stone," Rupert called back.

"Hurry. It'll be dark soon. I want the camp set up in one minute."

Rupert lifted the stone and turned to the pepper poet.

"I have to go."

"What about my story? I made you famous," the plant whined.

"Tell it to yourself," Rupert said, walking off. "I'm living my own story."

"Next time you want your boring food spicy, don't come looking to me," snapped the pepper poet, which then continued mumbling to itself.

Rupert completed the ring of rocks around the pond grass. Weaver returned from gathering various leaves, fruit and vines and sat down across from him.

"Keep your eye on that camper grass," he said, gesturing at the lump in the center of the fire ring. "It's just about ready."

"Ready to what?"

Before Weaver could respond, Rupert had his answer. From the center of the wad of grass came a little fountain of sparks. The sparks grew thicker and thicker until finally the entire pile erupted into a great warming fire.

"Cool!"

"Cool? No, hot," Weaver said. "Camper grass sets itself on fire when it dries. That'll burn all night. Then we put it back in the pond, and it will grow again."

"Boy, I can't wait to tell Squeem about all this."

Weaver divided the things he had gathered and handed half to Rupert.

"The blue fruit is a waterbustle—just pull off the stem and sip the liquid inside. The vine and the purple berries should fill you up."

"Thanks, Mr. Weaver."

Weaver nodded, and Rupert began eating.

They sat in silence as the fire crackled. It seemed to grow brighter as the sun set and allowed the darkness of night to cover all of Far-Myst. Rupert enjoyed the strange fruit and vines. The taste was like nothing he had ever eaten back in Graysland.

When he was done, he sat staring into the flames, throwing Weaver an occasional glance. The gardener never spoke a word. His thoughts were clearly about other things.

Rupert looked out past the circle of firelight into the darkness. The nightlight moss under the silverberry plant was glowing, attracting a small swarm of tiny insects that danced in its light. From deep in the gardens came strange sounds.

"What's making those sounds?" Rupert finally asked.

"Catfrogs and lolliwogs," Weaver mumbled.

Rupert had so many more questions but was afraid to say anything. Finally, he gathered enough nerve.

"Do you think Queen Chroma is okay?"

"I am sure she's fine."

"Why does Murkus want to make everything dull and boring?"

"Murkus doesn't want to make everything boring. Murkus wants to make everything like himself. Mean. Nasty. Angry."

"Why?"

"Why is the sun hot? Why is water wet?"

"I don't know. Just is."

"Exactly." Weaver tossed a frayed end of vine into the fire and watched it burn to cinders.

"Are you angry, too?"

Weaver shot Rupert a glance then turned back to the fire.

"That is my own business. All we need to concern ourselves with is getting you home."

"Why?"

"What do you mean why? You can't stay here."

"But Pie O'Sky brought me here to help."

Weaver smiled and shook his head.

"Pie O'Sky thinks everything can be fixed by childish imagination."

"Can't it?"

"Did it keep all the other children safe?" Weaver snapped. "They are probably all rotting in one of Murkus's filthy cells. Including my own children!"

Rupert was scared by the gardener's angry voice. Weaver saw it, took a deep breath and stood up. He looked at Rupert in silence a moment then took another deep breath and changed the subject.

"You should get some sleep. Tomorrow, we'll see if it's safe to go back to the castle. Otherwise, I'll have to take you to Flowseen. It's a small village, quite a hike away. There's a man there. A friend. He should be able to get you back to your Graysland place."

"He has a bagoon?"

"No. A bagoon is just a way to go from one place to another. The road can be traveled other ways."

"What do you mean?" Rupert asked, his forehead wrinkling with confusion.

"There are ways to use Imagining powers to create bagoons, or wagons, or even boats that can break through from one land to another."

"Break through what?"

"The mysterious walls that separate places. A bit beyond me. My friend understands these things better than I."

"Pie O'Sky does, too, right?"

"Yes, he does."

"I don't wanna go back through whatever wall there is between here and Graysland."

"Do you want your parents to worry?"

"They're boring."

"Boring or not, there's nothing more frightening than not knowing where your children are. Now, get to sleep."

Rupert crawled into the giant hollow bullfrogstool and made himself comfortable. The bottom of his fungus tent was very soft—much more comfortable than his bed at home.

He peered out through the opening and watched as Dream Weaver cleaned up the tiniest of crumbs left from their meal and tossed them all into the fire. Then Dream Weaver took a seat under a tree, folded his arms and stared into the dancing flames.

"Do you want to hear a story, Mr. Weaver?" Rupert asked.

"From your wonderful and powerful imagination?" Weaver growled, but he softened his harsh words with a little smile.

"No, from that plant with those hot-pepper things."

"The plant? The pepper poet plant?" Weaver asked with a deepening frown.

"Yes. He offered—"

"Mister Rupert Dullz, do I have to tie you down? I warned you. Don't touch any of the plants. It took me a lifetime to learn what they all do."

"But it offered—"

"I don't care if it forced your mouth open and jumped in—plants are complicated creatures. It takes study. It takes wisdom. Some of them can be very dangerous in the hands of a wet-behind-the-ears brat who thinks with his butt instead of his brain!"

Rupert sighed hard.

"Don't sigh. Listen."

"I was just doing what the—"

"Goodnight, Dullz," Weaver snapped.

Rupert pouted and made a few faces at the gardener on the sly. He rolled onto his back and shifted so he could see out the opening and peer up through the crisscrossing branches above. Many stars were shimmering, and they seemed brighter than he had ever known stars to be.

Despite Weaver's grumpy nature, despite the horrible wingers and the danger that was descending on Far-Myst, Rupert felt the excitement of this new world rumbling in his stomach and flowing with his blood. He found that when he closed his eyes many, many of the wondrous sights flashed through his mind in ways his thoughts had never done in Graysland. Colorful memories.

While his body was toasty warm from the living flesh of the bullfrog stool, he could feel a growing chill on his face. He watched Weaver pull his cloak tightly around his shoulders and hold his hands out to the fire. Rupert felt some sadness for the man and suddenly thought about his own family. He could almost hear the moaning snores and mumbling coming from his parent's bedroom. Was his grandmother hacking and coughing?

He smiled as great hope filled his heart. He would find a cure for the coffus. Somewhere in this peculiar land, there would be a cure.

In the far distance, the blackest of all storms was inching closer. It thickened and gathered with terrible purpose. It dripped with anger and distrust and left nothing but blandness and sadness in its wake.

Rupert was still snoring when Weaver filled his lungs with the first deep breath of the new day.

"Up on your feet, Dullz. None of this sleeping until the shadows shorten!"

He clapped his hands and headed to the pond to splash some water on his face. He froze in his tracks. His eyes widened, and he gasped.

"In the name of my own brood, do my eyes fail me?"

The Seven Spectral Oaks stood gray before him. All the red and the orange, all the yellow, green and blue, all the indigo and violet were drained from their leaves. Bland gray foliage rustled gently in the early-morning breeze.

"Rupert, wake up! We have to leave here immediately."

Rupert mumbled and protested, his eyes tightly shut against the incoming beams of sunlight. Weaver wasn't playing games. He reached into the bullfrog stool and tugged on the boy's arm sharply.

"Get up! The Spectral Oaks have all gone gray!"

Rupert opened his eyes and sat up.

"But I thought you said only the violet one would go gray?"

"I know what I said."

Rupert stepped from the tent, and Weaver reached in and removed the small leaf of silverberry. Almost instantly, the bullfrog stool wiggled and shook then shrank back down to its original size.

Rupert stared with saddened eyes at the Seven Oaks.

"They look like they belong in Graysland."

"Rupert, I need to check on the castle. I fear the worst. You must promise me you will stay put. Do not move a step. I'll be back in less then an hour."

Rupert could hear how worried Weaver was.

"Why can't I come with you to the castle?"

"Because it may be too dangerous. You're safe here. The wingers hate the Garden. You must give me your word that you'll sit by the pond and stay put. Do *not* wander off."

Rupert nodded repeatedly.

"I want to hear you say it. *Mr. Weaver, I promise I will stay put until your return.*"

"I promise I'll stay put, Mr. Weaver," Rupert said sincerely.

Weaver nodded. "The water from the small stream that washes into the pond is good to drink. The red berries on that fillengo bush make a good breakfast. Other than that, don't eat or touch anything."

"I won't."

"I'll be right back."

Dream Weaver headed back along the path they had used the day before. Rupert watched as he vanished into the trees and bushes then strolled over to the pond and knelt. He dipped his fingers into the cool water and saw his reflection.

He didn't see the nightwinger sitting in the highest branch of one of the seven Spectral Oaks, staring down at him with a terrible smirk.

Chapter 9

Wingers in the Way

There was no time to waste, so Weaver didn't take the well-worn paths that snaked through the Garden of Dreams. He pushed through walls of shrubs and mazes of tree trunks and thick vines, being ever careful not to damage any of the precious plants.

As he climbed a small hill above a clearing, a whispering pine caught his attention with a sharp *psst! psst!*

"What is it, Sunwood?" Weaver asked the tall, ancient tree with a thick white trunk that reflected the morning sun and gave him his name.

"Heard a tale in the breeze this morning," Sunwood whispered. "Like fish scales on a bird, it was an oddity."

"I have no time for riddles. Get to the point," Weaver demanded.

"Everstood Castle no longer shines," the tree reported sadly. "It just sits there like an old dead log."

Weaver's mouth curled into a tight frown. He could not believe it. He *would* not. This had to be a false rumor. The air was full of them.

Far-Myst had always been a land of practical jokes and tall tales. Stories would pass from person to tree, plant to bird, and they would grow taller and less practical with each telling.

No! Weaver thought. *This cannot be true.*

He raced on across the field of stubby dragon's-beard grass and entered the wooded area that bordered the garden's eastern edge. Keeping his steps quick but silent, he moved like a night fox to the ancient stone wall that surrounded the Garden of Dreams.

Weaver climbed to the wall's top, using the thick stems of sentinel vine that grew on it like a ladder. He cautiously peered over and gazed across the wide-open expanse to the eastern face of the castle. He could not believe what his eyes were seeing. He felt like crying.

Rupert filled his cupped hands with the water from the stream and sipped it. It was cold as ice and tasted great. As he reached down for another handful, he heard a familiar voice.

"Hey! Kid!" It was the pepper poet plant.

Rupert turned to the plant, which sat waving in a breeze some distance away.

"What?"

"What did you think of the story?"

"Your story got me in trouble with Mr. Weaver. He got mad at me for eating one of your peppers."

"Weaver's a smart guy, but not too blessed in the smiles department, if you know what I mean," the plant commented.

Rupert frowned and approached it.

"He's sad because his kids are gone. You would be, too, if somebody came and swiped all your peppers."

"No, I wouldn't. I *want* my peppers swiped. That way, my stories can be read-tasted. Unless it's someone like you. Too scared."

"I'm not scared. There's something bad going on in Far-Myst."

"Ohhhh! Look who's a sudden expert on Far-Myst? How long have you been here, kid?"

"Almost a day."

"Wow, a whole day! Maybe I should write a special speech honoring the new expert in Far-Myst history," the pepper poet said with a chuckle.

"I'm not an expert," Rupert defended himself. "I just want to be of help."

"I have one tale in particular that just might be of interest to you and Mr. Charm School Dream Weaver."

"Why?"

"Well, I don't know if I should say. Little pitcher plants have big ears, as the saying goes. But I can give you a hint. This story is quick and fancy."

"Quick and fancy? So, big deal. You're just trying to tempt me."

"Alright, have it your way. I'll just give it to the next kid that comes along. One that isn't so D-U-L-L!"

"I'm not dull!" Rupert frowned and snatched the pinkish-purple pepper. "My name is Rupert Starbright."

"Of course you ain't dull. Now, eat the pepper and tell me the story."

Rupert pouted and lifted the little colorful fruit to his lips and sniffed it.

"Must you sniff your food?" Pepper Poet asked in disgust.

Before Rupert could respond, a shadow fell over him, and there was a sudden stench of dead mice and the cracking of terrible wings. A sinister laugh broke the air. He froze as a nightwinger landed before him, great strings of drool dripping from its fangs.

"What an unexpected plot twist!" cried Pepper Poet.

Rupert stared into the red eyes of the beast. He wanted to run, but his feet seemed to be frozen in concrete.

"Hello, child," hissed the nightwinger.

Weaver stared in stunned silence. The old pine's whispered rumors had been right. Everstood Castle no longer shone like a trillion jewels. It stood like a hunk of coal.

Black.

Dull.

It had become a giant shadow.

There were no local folks walking around laughing or selling produce or sharing jokes. Only an army of nightwingers patrolled the grounds. All the trees along the fancy walkways and every flower and blade of grass and leaf of shrub had turned gray.

Even the sky, although clear of clouds, had its normal blue taken from it.

A large patch of ugly grayness hovered over the residence of Queen Chroma. Murkus's dark powers were draining the life from Everstood.

Is the queen okay? Are all the folks of Far-Myst safe inside?

Weaver had no time to think about such things. He had only one concern—Rupert. Queen Chroma had left the boy in his charge. He jumped from the wall to return to the clearing.

The horrid grimace of a nightwinger, its teeth flashing, leered at him when he turned back toward the garden. The creature had its wings spread to block Weaver's path.

"Hellooo, Gardener!" the monster spat.

Weaver frowned and slipped the Illuminor dagger from his belt. The nightwinger pounced, knocking him to the ground, sending the dagger flying from his hand.

Rupert trembled as the nightwinger crept closer. He could smell its terrible stink and feel the chill that came off the thing's body.

"What do you want from me?" he said, his voice shaky.

"Nothing, my good lad. I just want to take you on a ride. A ride high into the air. Come, boy, let me take you."

"No!"

As the winger dived for him, Rupert took a step backwards and slipped. It was a lucky accident. Not as agile on its feet as in the air, the winger landed off-balance and ended up face-first on the ground.

Rupert ran. He had no clue where he was running to or even that his legs were moving. He just felt the wind on his face and saw the plants and trees whizzing by in a blur of blended colors. His heart pounded faster than it ever had.

A scream of anger shot across the garden like a cannonball. The winger was mad and was back on its feet, flapping its wings and racing towards him. Luckily for Rupert, the many trees made it hard for the beast to fully spread its wings, and it was forced to use its legs.

He was afraid to look over his shoulder, but the sound of its footsteps was growing louder. Closer. That now-familiar stink of dead mouse tickled his nose. His legs felt like gooey noodles. Gooey noodles with hoopaleaf sauce like his mother would make him. He wished he were back home in his boring kitchen eating that sloppy, tasteless mass of dough and stick-flavored gravy.

The road grew steeper as he darted up the rocky path that led through avenues of tall blue pines with silver cones shaped like bells that jingled in the breeze. Rupert wasn't sure he could take another step. His legs would soon collapse. He would be taken by the winger to places far away and terrible.

He closed his eyes and pushed on. The winger's breath and growling voice were mere inches from his ears. It let out another scream.

Without warning, Rupert felt his legs give way, and the world went black.

Weaver and the winger rolled on the muddy ground, each trying to get the upper hand in their wrestling match. The creature's claws dug into the gardener's shoulder. Weaver could see, from the corner of his eye, the Illuminor lying on the ground some ten feet away. He had to get it back!

"No use, plant man," the winger sneered. "You have lost. Your little friend is on his way to the hands of Lord Murkus, where all the other children are."

The scream of another winger came from deep in the garden.

"Ha! My comrade has succeeded in his mission. The boy is ours."

"No! Rupert!"

Using every ounce of strength he had, Weaver pushed with his feet and flipped his body up, sending the winger tumbling heels over butt. He turned to the dagger and leaped for it. His hand fell mere inches from its fancy, shiny opal-and-silver handle as the winger dived atop him.

"Forget it, Gardener. The boy is gone. You lose!"

Weaver heard none of the winger's taunting. He felt for the dangling end of the vine that trailed from the wall and grabbed it. He pulled on it, scraping along the ground, inching ever closer to the Illuminor.

The winger, thinking it had won, laughed and flapped its wings victoriously then raised a hand and extended its six knife-like claws.

"Goodbye, plant lover!" The winger's vicious hand swept down.

Weaver made his move. Using the tips of his fingers, he managed to grasp the handle of the dagger and slide it towards him. When his entire hand was around the hilt, it came alive in a glittering display of rainbow light.

The nightwinger screamed in horror, jumping off Weaver's back.

"Drat you, gardener!"

Weaver jumped to his feet and swung the Illuminor at the beast. A spray of colored light flew forward and sent the winger fleeing to the skies. Another cry came from the garden. Weaver raced off.

Rupert was in a dark and cool place. It smelled of moist soil and rotted leaves, much like his yard in Graysland, and for a moment, it calmed him.

Then he noticed the soft orange glow just above his head. It was an orange moss, glowing like embers. A voice spoke, deep and gentle.

"You seem to be in some sort of danger, young human."

"Where am I?"

"You have slipped into the entrance of the home of the molerabbit family. They're out at the moment, collecting nuts and berries."

"Who are you?"

"You're taking shelter under my roots. Who else would be speaking? The soil? The mind's-eye moss?"

"In this place, it seems like anything is possible."

"My name is Pinefore. There seems to be a creature of a very foul nature hunting you."

"It's a nightwinger," Rupert whispered.

"I have heard rumors of such things. Never have they shown the courage to enter the Garden of Dreams. They must be getting bolder."

Deep growls and the smell of rotting mice entered through the mesh of roots from outside. In the tiny slash of light, he saw the shadowy shape of the winger's bony hand reaching inside. Rupert held his breath and scootched as far from its awful clutching as he could.

The hand stretched closer, and the hoarse voice of the winger dribbled into the underground den like dripsludge.

"Come on out, boy. I will not hurt you. No need to hide from me."

With each word came the stink of the winger's breath.

The mind's-eye moss began glowing brighter.

Weaver entered the clearing and looked toward the pond. Rupert was nowhere in sight. His keen eyes spotted the small pinkish-purple pepper lying on the ground. He picked it up and peered off into the dense foliage. He spotted the dark form of the winger off in the distance, peering into a hole beneath a great pine tree.

"What mischief are you up to in there?" the winger asked, pulling its hand back and peering in with its blood-red eyes. "What is that nasty light?"

Rupert glanced at the glowing moss. The winger reached in again.

Rupert grabbed a handful of the mind's-eye moss and slapped in against the hand. The creature jumped back in fear, and its terrible scream echoed across the garden.

"Disgusting child!" the creature cried.

Heavy footsteps approached. Rupert's heart was pounding in his throat. He grabbed another chunk of the moss and waited. There was the sound of a scuffle followed by a cry of terror. He peered out the narrow opening.

The winger was backing off. Its wings opened, and there was the sound of heavy flapping. Then all went silent. For a moment, Rupert was afraid to breathe.

Another hand shot into the hole and took him by the front of his shirt. Rupert slapped it with the moss, but the grip was firm and pulled him from the hole like a farmer picking a carrot. He punched and kicked the stocky figure.

"Relax, Rupert, it's me. Relax!" Weaver said, putting him back on his own feet.

Rupert looked up and exhaled hard.

"Weaver!"

"I thought I told you to stay by the pond?"

"I did. That winger came and—"

"You picked another pepper," Weaver said, pulling the small pinkish-purple pepper from his pocket. "And you damaged the mind's-eye moss."

"But it scared the winger away."

Weaver's frown softened.

"I'll admit that was quick thinking."

"What happened at the castle?"

"We have to leave here. Soon, all the colors will drain from Far-Myst."

"What are they gonna do?"

"We'll worry about our own problems. Yours is going back to Graysland."

"Maybe I can help, like Pie O'Sky said."

"*You* are going home. I'm going to gather up some essentials. Supplies. It's going to take about three days. You will stay in sight. You will do what I say. Once we exit the gardens, we'll be traveling in dangerous territory. Do you hear me, Mister Dullz?"

Rupert nodded, although he wasn't happy. Weaver put the pepper back into his cloak pocket and led him back to the pond.

Chapter 10

Two Walls

"I've never seen such dark clouds before," Rupert said as he peered from a clearing. "We'll be heading directly towards them."

They stood atop a hill that offered a view across a wide misty valley. Painted against the sky, as far away as a distant memory, stood the Feign Mountains, faded like the words of a long-forgotten song.

Weaver settled his leather-and-canvas bag's strap across his shoulder. It was jam-packed with supplies. Rupert wore his own pack, made from the large cloth-like leaves of the satchel tree, that Weaver had made.

They had enough waterbustle plants to give them fresh water for three days. Weaver was sure they could live off the land but had packed enough camper grass and edible jerky bark to keep them warm and fed in case of emergencies.

"Enough sightseeing, Dullz. I want to make it to the Walls before nightfall. I want us both to have a good night's sleep before we enter the Wildness."

"That sounds very unboring," Rupert said with a grin.

"Unboring, indeed. After a taste of the Wildness of Far-Myst, with the clouds of Murkus gathering, you will dream of your uneventful life in Graysland," Weaver warned.

Rupert trotted down from the hill and joined Weaver back on the trail. He kept tripping over rocks and splashing across small streams and inlets. A familiar sound rang in his ears, a *crunch-crunch* he could feel beneath his feet. He looked down at the carpet of dead fallen leaves.

"I didn't think leaves died in Far-Myst."

"Of course they do. Some trees drop their leaves in the warm months and others in the cold," Weaver explained as he stopped before a tree with a thick, twisted trunk. "This is a fortune tree."

Rupert let his head fall back and gazed up at the wide, arching branches that sprouted little colorful buds.

"There are so many different plants and trees, how do you remember them all?" he asked, very impressed.

"It's my job," Weaver grunted. "Go ahead. Pick up one of the leaves and open it."

Confused, Rupert reached down and grabbed a handful of leaves.

"Just one. Not right to take more."

He dropped the load and scanned the choices. He picked up a bright red-and-gold leaf and discovered it was folded into a small container. He could feel there was an object inside. He shook it near his ear. Weaver smiled slightly.

"That's good. There's a fortune seed inside. Open it."

Rupert cracked the dry shell of the leaf and let the seed fall onto his palm. It was a little ball, light-brown in color.

"What do I do with it?"

"It'll begin to glow bright red, like an ember, if forces unfriendly to the imagination are near," Weaver explained.

"How does it know?"

"It just does."

Rupert nodded and put the seed in his pocket then followed the gardener down the path.

They walked without talking for a while, the sounds of the wind and the birds drifting in and out of their private thoughts. Rupert suddenly stopped, staring at the side of the path.

"What's wrong?" Weaver asked.

"What's that?"

Rupert knelt down and pointed to a strange object partially buried in the soil between two shrubs. Weaver stepped closer, and his eyes filled with sadness.

"A lost and rotting dream."

The thing was a lighthearted assembly of color-ful gears, fake eyeballs, large wheels and feathery wings. It was coated in weeks'-worth of dust and was rotting like old leaves. Weaver took hold of one of the gears and pulled. It crumbled like a stale cookie.

"This was once alive in a child's imagination." he mourned.

"Is this like those things in the museum? Pie O'Sky said that they sometimes appeared far from the child who thought of it."

Weaver nodded and stood up and filled his lungs with air.

"Must have been imagined by the last child to be free in Far-Myst. Poor child is probably..." He looked away and couldn't finish the thought.

Rupert stood up, and a hopeful light sparked in his eyes.

"Maybe this was just Imagined. A few minutes ago. Maybe the kids are still Imagining stuff even though that creep Murkus is trying to stop them."

Weaver smiled ever so slightly and tussled Rupert's hair.

"Glad to see hope alive somewhere. It's just about gone in my heart."

He headed off, and Rupert followed close behind.

"What are your children's names?" Rupert asked.

Weaver looked skyward, and a distant smile formed on his face, although his eyes became wet.

"Quixotic and Fancimore. My boy's about your age. Bigger. Sturdy. My little Fancy is eight."

"Those are definitely not boring names like Rupert Dullz."

"What happened to that Starbright name the queen introduced you with?"

"I copied that name from this man in Graysland who used his imagination to make just-because books. Mookie Starbright. I like his name better than mine. Boring old Dullz."

"Nothing boring about it, Dullz. It's your name. Be proud of it."

Rupert doubted he could.

"When was the last time you saw your kids?"

"*Kids* are baby goats. Fancy and Quix are my *children*," Weaver snapped as the rare smile on his face dissolved away like chalk in the rain. He stiffened and marched on. "Enough talking, lad. Let's go."

Something about the names of Weaver's children rang a bell in Rupert's mind. He tried to think why that might be as he walked.

The main courtyard of the Dark Keep of Murkus was a wide, open-air field of dark, hard soil. It was filled with hundreds of children. They stood in neat rows beside holes dug in the ground. Each held a small shovel, and buckets sat by dirty, bare feet so caked with mud it appeared the children were wearing boots.

Piles of soil sat at the end of each row, waiting to be taken somewhere else in the many rusted wheelbarrows that were scattered about. The entire yard was surrounded by high stone walls with drooling nightwingers marching on them.

There was complete silence from the children. They looked very tired, and there was not a smile on any of the hundreds of little faces.

Murkus stepped out onto a high porch that jutted from the southern wall of the keep. His sickly-looking moist white skin reflected the dull light like the skin of a giant worm. He lifted his arms high and began to speak in a powerful voice that boomed across the yard.

"Small ones from Far-Myst! The colors of your homeland are fading. Soon, nothing but bland grayness will be all that the remaining residents can behold.

"You are the lucky ones. You have been chosen to live lives of pure dullness and boredom in service to me. Be honored. The holes you will dig until the end of your days will be a constant reminder of dullness and toil. These are the things that will make you powerful, not that Imagining nonsense, which only makes you weak!"

There was some grumbling and sounds of disagreement. From somewhere in the crowd a voice, sounding tired but sure, called out, "Go piss in your hat, Murkus!"

Murkus smiled for a second then spoke to the winger beside him.

"Flyer! Take that smart-mouthed little brat to the dark cells."

The nightwinger took to the air as cries of terror filled the yard. It swooped down and snatched the boy who had dared to challenge Murkus. He was carried up and into one of the many tunnel openings that lined the walls.

The noise of the crowd was quickly hushed by Murkus's voice.

"Does anyone else want to join him?" He cocked his head back and forth and heard nothing but the wind. "I need a volunteer. The bravest child. The most loyal. The one who will relish the honor of serving my vision for your world."

Confused glances were tossed about, and there were soft whispers.

One boy who stood head and shoulders above the dirty-faced girl beside him smiled ever so slightly. He was about eleven or twelve but had a look of strength and determination in his eyes more like that of a grown-up.

He turned to the boy on his other side.

"Hear that, Xerks? A volunteer."

Xerks was a wide-eyed boy with a wild mass of blond hair that stood out as if electricity were flowing through him. His smile was filled with green-tinted teeth, and his cheeks were flushed and muddy.

"Yes, Quix, volunteers for Murkus."

A quick slap to the back of his head silenced them both as a passing nightwinger leered at them.

"No blabbering, runts!" the winger hissed.

The girl threw her arms around Quix's waist and buried her face against his stomach. The winger gave her a nasty smile.

"Are you afraid of me, sweet potato?

"Leave her alone, creep," Quix warned without fear, "or my shovel will dig a new hole in your head."

The winger laughed.

"There is a child wandering Far-Myst," Murkus continued. "A child from a distant place. I believe him to be a spy. A spy who thinks he can invade my land and take you all as his prisoners. That cannot be allowed to happen. I want one of you to find this little creature and make friends with him. Discover the truth of his mission."

Quix and Xerks looked at each other and smiled wickedly.

"Murkus rules!" Xerks said with a drooling smirk. Quix nodded and lifted his arm into the air.

"No! Quix, you can't! Daddy will be hurt!" the little girl protested.

"Fancy! Shh! I'll do want I want. No little sister of mine will have anything to say about it. Where was our father when we needed him? He's no longer a father of mine."

Murkus spotted the hand waving over the crowd. A second joined it as Xerks raised his.

"Yes! Two brave and loyal lads will serve my need. Wingers! Take these minions of Murkus to my lair. Now, back to the holes. All of you."

With that, he turned and marched off to the heavy, drum-like sound of his own bootsteps.

Two wingers did as ordered, and as Quix and Xerks were lifted, little Fancy could do nothing but watch, teary-eyed.

Slog guided Quix and Xerks into the private chamber of Murkus and peered in nervously. Murkus sat on his throne of filth, tapping his fingers on the arm with impatience as he stared through the dusty window.

"Don't stand there peeking in, Slog! Bring my new friends in like proper guests!"

"Yes, yes, milord! Here they are. Lovely young things, they are. Oh, yes, yes! Their names are Quix and Xerks. What perfect names, don't you think, milord?"

"Slog. Leave. Immediately," Murkus commanded.

Slog slunk out and waited in the hall as the two boys entered the lair. Quix stood with arms folded, staring blank-faced at the horrible throne. Xerks's gaze darted about like a bat in a closet. A wild smile filled his face.

"Which one of you is Quix?" Murkus asked in a low rumble of a voice.

"I am," Quix said as he stepped forward. "Quix Weaver."

"I know your father. He is a favorite of the queen."

Quix nodded slightly but said nothing.

"Why do you wish to help me? Aren't your loyalties with Queen Chroma?"

Quix tightened his lips and lifted his chin. His eyes seem to spark with anger.

"The queen is ignorant. Imagination is nothing but lies and causes nothing but destruction of the mind. The only way to save those fools in Far-Myst is to end the childish Imaginings. Things should be black-and-white. Color just confuses it all. My father could never understand that. All he cares about are his plants."

"You are a smart boy," Murkus drooled, and turned to Xerks. "How about you?"

"Me?" Xerks smirked. "I hate all grownups, and the kids out there digging those holes are idiots. They say they don't like you because you're bad. What's so great about *good*? *Good* is for fools. My parents were good. What did it ever do for them? They wanted me to use my Imaginings for *good*. I Imagined something called Darkledroons. Big black moths that could do all sorts of things. They ended up..."

Xerks's face tightened, and he seemed to be having trouble getting the end of his sentence out. Murkus glared at him.

"Ended up what?" the giant probed.

Xerks swallowed hard and lifted his chin high.

"Ended up turning on my parents. This *good* Imagining was not so good. Turned their minds into mush. Filled them with so much fear they…" He swallowed hard. "…died."

"Your dark Imaginings may come in handy, young Xerks," Murkus said with a terrible smile as he stood up. "I would like to see these Darkledroons of yours."

Quix studied the large figure. Murkus was even taller up close than he had imagined.

Murkus stepped to the window and pulled down a shade. On it was a map that glowed from the light shining behind it. Quix could tell immediately it was a map of Far-Myst.

"A new child has appeared. He was brought here by Pie O'Sky from an unknown land. There are whispers beginning to spread he may have great strength. Strength to make *good* Imaginings. There has even been talk this boy may be the *Stella Lumina* mentioned in the old tales."

"What is the Stella Lumina?" Xerks wondered.

"You should know your history, boy. The coming of the Stella Lumina was told around the campfires of the ancients. Silly tales of a child with such a powerful imagination he can even give adults back *their* Imagining power. Nonsense!"

Murkus began laughing loud and mockingly. His laughter died down, and an evil glare sparked in his eyes.

"Rumors have also begun to emerge that he may be the first of an army. An army of brats who would dare attempt to conquer me."

"No one can conquer you, Murkus," Xerks said with a pump of his fist.

Murkus's eyes flared a moment. No one ever interrupted him without severe punishment. However, he forced a smile and placed his wet, slimy hand on Xerks's face. Xerks tried to control the shiver that spread from the touch of the lifeless skin.

"You will honor me." Murkus slapped the map with his palm. "Somewhere in the wilds of Far-Myst, the brat is wandering with that plant-loving father of yours, Quix. He has obviously abandoned his own son to protect another boy. But you will show him your own justice. Then, you will make friends with this boy and learn the secrets of his plot."

Quix nodded with a blank face, but there was fire in his eyes.

"Now, get back to work. The flyers will take you into the Wildness when I give the order. Slog! Take them back to the yard."

Slog slipped in, bowing and nodding.

"Yes. Yes, oh, yes. Good boys. I mean, bad boys. Follow me. Follow me, my good-bad boys."

Xerks and Quix bowed to Murkus and followed Slog out.

Murkus listened as the footsteps faded into the bowels of his keep. He stroked his chin and grinned. He went over to an opening in the rocky wall, reached in and retrieved a brown oval object. It was an egg—a large one that covered his palm completely. Its dull shell had tiny cracks and splotches of black across it. He stared at it, gazing into its surface like a wizard into a crystal ball.

"What do you think of them, my love?" he asked the egg. "Should I trust them?"

He pressed his ear ever so gently against the egg, and his expression changed over and over.

"I agree. The Xerks child is an imbecile. Too wild. Careless. But I enjoy his anger and hatred. The gardener's son—he boils inside. Even angrier than the other. He may prove to be a pawn with the heart of a knight.

"But you are right. I must watch him closely. I can see the pride and certainty in his eyes. Matters not. They will all be crushed once I am done with them."

Murkus returned the egg into the hole and sat on his throne.

Chapter 11

Walls on the March

Weaver hiked Rupert through the Garden of Dreams with little rest. When they climbed the steeper parts of the garden, where the fountain cactus grew, Rupert's legs grew weary, but he marveled at the fanciful water displays that sprayed from the spiny nozzles of the cacti. They crossed the wide Plain of Wild Flowers, whose nonstop party filled the air with song.

Finally, the distinct edges of the wall that enclosed the garden could be seen through the trees, winding around the land like a great stone snake. Beyond it was the infinite wilderness of Far-Myst. The *Wildness*, most people called it.

Another two hours of hiking was behind them by the time they came to the Wall of the Garden of Dreams. Twice the height of Weaver, it was built of thick gray, red and brown stones of different sizes. Some were as big as a couch!

The rocks were ancient, and a healthy coat of moss filled all the places where one stone joined another. Along the base of the wall, vines slithered and roots from countless plants and trees poked from the soil.

Weaver looked like he could have marched all night, but he knew Rupert needed to rest before his legs gave out. He stopped in a small clearing.

"Take one waterbustle and one strip of jerky bark from your pack," he ordered.

Rupert dug through his bag. When he had what he needed, Weaver took the pack from him and hung it with his own on the broken branch of an elephant tree. He gave one of the four giant trunks a pat, and the branch lifted up into the canopy, taking the bags with it.

"That's to keep it safe from any wandering animals. A trumpet wolf or a laughing bear gets a whiff of anything edible, and they'll steal it before you can say 'Pie O'Sky.'"

"There are wolves and bears around here?" Rupert asked, wide-eyed.

"There are hundreds of kinds of animals living in the Wildness. They usually stay on that side of the wall, run off when they hear people coming. But you never know."

"I hope we see something."

"Let's get the camp set up. You know the drill. Get the fire ring built."

"I'm hungry."

"You'll eat after the camp is set. Move."

Rupert's shoulders slumped, but he went about gathering stones, quickly building a ring after shoving aside the carpet of pine needles that covered the clearing. He was exhausted from the hours of walking, but the quicker the ring was built, the quicker he knew he would eat and get some sleep.

Weaver took a clump of camper grass he had stored in a water bustle and set it on the ground to dry. He began collecting firewood, and in a matter of minutes, a warming fire was aglow, battling the cold air of the coming night.

Rupert struggled to bite off a piece of jerky bark. He pulled and yanked until finally the strip tore and he fell back head over heels.

"The dangers of eating jerky bark," Weaver said with a grin.

"It's a teeth-yanker," Rupert agreed as he got up. "Tastes pretty good, though. Better than splage. That's what we eat all the time at home."

"So, do you have a large family back there in Graysland?" Weaver asked.

Rupert smiled a little as he thought about them. He wondered again about his grandmother and how much she was coughing.

"I live with my mom, dad and grandmother. My grandma is sick. She has the coffus. I was hoping there might be a cure here for her. Something that imagination could make."

"What's the coffus?"

"It's when you cough a lot."

"Well, never heard coughing called the coffus. Maybe someone in Flowseen has an idea. Some smart folk in that part of Far-Myst."

"That would be great."

They sat in silence a moment, and Rupert noticed that, except for a few sips of water, Weaver wasn't eating.

"Shouldn't you eat some jerky, too?" he suggested.

"Never mind what I eat. You just finish your ration for tonight. Going to need energy for tomorrow when we go over the wall and into the Wildness."

"You'll need energy, too," Rupert pointed out.

Weaver ignored him.

Rupert studied the faraway look in the gardener's eyes.

"I'm sure your kids—children—are eating fine. And I don't think they would want you to starve yourself for them. You have to be even stronger so you can get them back."

Weaver glared at him. Rupert looked away and was expecting to be scolded for such a bold statement.

"You have some wisdom in you, Dullz. That sounded like something my Quix would say."

"Does he want to be a gardener, too?"

"No. He has his mind set on being a mapper. Travel the far-distant reaches of Far-Myst never seen by the human eye. Map the lands for those who follow. Every boy his age wants to be a mapper. Wants adventure. Travel. It's in the blood of the young. Like the Imagining."

"Do adults here get all boring like they do in Graysland?" Rupert asked.

"I can't speak for any others but myself. I had many young years of Imagining ability. Then I traveled more than I care to say. I've been all around the Wildness. Some places I hope I never see again."

"Were you a mapper?"

"Yes. And other things as well."

"Like what?"

Weaver looked away, and Rupert took another bite off the jerky strip.

"I was one of the Twelve," Weaver said softly.

"Twelve what?"

"We were a special group of knights."

"A knight? What's a knight?"

"A soldier, like the Palace Guards. Sort of."

"Sort of?"

"We were also called the Illuminorians. We protected Far-Myst from those who would use the Imaginings for evil. The Twelve were much busier ages ago when adults still had the power."

"That when you got that knife? The Illuminor?"

Weaver nodded. "I was part of the last group of Twelve. One of the youngest."

"How does the Illuminor work?"

"They project good thoughts at those with dark ones. They do not kill or harm in any way, but creatures like the wingers are so caught up in darkness, it pains their cold hearts to feel love or good or creative thoughts. It holds up a mirror to their dark hearts and lets them see for themselves how much change they need."

"Where are the rest of the Twelve?"

"The Twelve was dissolved, and now we teach, or spend our days lounging in retirement."

"Or gardening," Rupert added.

Weaver nodded with a smile.

"Most are far away, teaching in other towns. Besides me, there are three near here. Whim Sungazer teaches at the school in Everstood. Summit Wonder lives in a little village called Story. And Kelna Myndpath, who lives in Flowseen."

"That's who we're going to see?" Rupert asked.

"Yes. She spends much of her time with her family living a simple farm life. She was an expert in Pathfinding. It's the same special Imagining power Pie O'Sky's bagoon uses to travel to other lands."

Rupert nodded and studied the thoughtful, far-off smile on Weaver's face.

"When did you become a gardener?"

A strange sadness turned down the smile.

"It's getting late. You'll need your sleep tonight. I wish there was a bullfrog stool or a lushrom for you to sleep on but there isn't. You'll have to sleep in the night air and under the stars."

"Cool!" Rupert exclaimed, excited by such an unboring idea.

Weaver smiled and took off his cloak. He handed it to Rupert.

"Cool, indeed. Maybe *cold*. Here, this will cut down on the nighttime chill."

"Thanks. But what about you?"

Weaver answered with his usual stern look. Rupert smiled.

"I know. I know. *Don't worry about you*," he said, mimicking Weaver's deep voice.

He found an especially thick pile of pine needles and lay down, throwing the cloak over him. The heat from the fire and the calm winds promised a comfortable night's sleep. He watched the shadows of the forest, thrown against the wall, dance with the flickering flames.

Weaver propped himself against one of the four trunks of the elephant tree and stared into the fire.

"So, who built that wall?"

"No one. It built itself."

"Huh?"

"It sprang, like a living thing, from the stream that circled the garden ages ago. The stream was called the Flow Ring."

"What was the wall for?"

"Legend tells that the lands of the garden are special. The wall, they say, assembled itself, formed from the imagination of the stream. It wasn't really protecting anything but rather marking it off as special. They say that as long as the wall remains, the Garden of Dreams will be the best protection against those who wish to destroy Far-Myst."

"Like Murkus?"

"Yes." Weaver frowned.

"What's on the other side of the wall, Mr. Weaver?"

"I told you. The Wildness. Endless. As far as the eye can see. All the way to the Feign Mountains and beyond."

"I can't wait to see it all," Rupert said, his voice fading off into a wide-mouthed yawn.

"Ya think so? What would you do if you came face-to-face with a giant ghost dog in the Drowning Woods?"

Rupert did not reply. The sound of his snoring filled the night.

Weaver's eyes hung like wet towels as well. He was fighting a sleep that had to come. He needed to rest a few hours and recharge his energy for the coming day of hiking across the unpredictable lands of the Wildness.

No one ever knew what to expect when venturing away from the friendly roads and towns nestled around the Everstood region. And, as a chill rode on the air from that terrible distant storm, he feared the future was even less certain than ever.

He let his eyes close and drifted off.

Something snapped Weaver's eyes back open. A sound like the grinding squeal of a large rock being dragged across a cobblestone street broke the quiet of the night. Soon, an entire chorus of dragging-rock sounds filled the air.

He turned to the wall and could only stare wide-eyed. One by one, the great ancient stones were reshaping themselves into stone figures! Arms and legs sprouted, and square heads popped out of rocky shoulders. Some had beards of thick green moss.

The stone people began marching off into the night.

"Rupert!" Weaver called out. "Wake up!"

He stood and approached the wall. The stone people treated him as if he were not there. He heard some of the Stone Folk speak as they trudged off to unknown places in the Wildness.

"We must follow Cornerstood."

"Dullz, wake up. We have to leave. Now!" Weaver said. He gave Rupert's legs a soft kick.

Rupert rolled onto his side and gasped at the sight.

"Who are they?"

"The stones of the wall," Weaver said sadly. "They're leaving the garden."

"Where are they going?" Rupert was still half-asleep and not quite sure if he wasn't simply dreaming.

"I haven't a clue. Looks like into the Wildness," Weaver said in awe. "We can't stay here."

"Why not?"

"Why not? Even in Far-Myst, walls don't come apart stone by stone and march off into the night like some parade, lad! Do they do so where you come from?"

"No. Walls are as dull as everything else in Graysland."

Weaver patted one trunk of the elephant tree, and it graciously lowered the packs on its nose-like branch. Weaver went to work putting out the fire, tossing handfuls of soil on it. He threw both packs over his shoulder and looked at Rupert, who was asleep again.

"Mr. Dullz!" Weaver shouted. "Up, I say!"

He reached down and whipped his cloak from Rupert. Rupert mumbled again and groggily opened his eyes. He caught the full force of Weaver's angry and impatient stare.

"You get to your stinking feet now. You have already caused me great delays in helping my own children. I am sure the queen needs me. I need to get you back home, you little pain in the rump, so I can tend to important things!"

Rupert stood up. He reached for his pack.

"I have it," Weaver said.

Rupert took it anyway.

"I can carry my own bag. I'm not gonna be any more bother to you, Mr. Weaver. I'm sorry I caused so many problems."

Weaver said nothing. He scanned the campsite one more time. He turned to Rupert, and his gaze softened.

"I'm hoping we can at least make it to the Elderwind Ruins."

"Whatever," mumbled Rupert.

Weaver led Rupert past the endless line of marching stone and into the Wildness of Far-Myst.

Chapter 12

Can You Imagine?

The queen's study in the western wing of Everstood Castle was lit by the glow of three candles. Three faces reflected the yellow light, each person staring into the darkness beyond the candlelight with eyes filled with anticipation. Queen Chroma was one of the three, and although the light showed the tired droop of her eyes, deep within them a fire of hope still sparkled.

Rona Piper sat beside her. She was a young woman with a head full of blond curls tied back to reveal a soft, pretty, pale face. She had a couple of pimples on her cheeks and forehead that made her appear five years younger than her twenty. She was the best flutist in all of Far-Myst and played with the Royal Orchestra.

Sitting beside her was a large man with skin the color of maple syrup and black hair in a single thick braid that fell across his shoulder and down his wide chest. He sported a thick black mustache that was curled and tipped with ruby beads. His name was Whim Sungazer, and he ran the Ever-stood School of Mindmatter Practices. One of the remaining Illuminorians, he taught the most imaginative children of Far-Myst the ancient ways of making the most of the powers of their minds and ways to extend the ability beyond childhood. Although only a handful had managed even a little success, his knowledge was greatly respected in all of Far-Myst. He was a trusted advisor to Queen Chroma.

"Try it again, Rona," Sungazer said softly.

Rona lifted a small silver flute to her lips, closed her eyes and began playing a series of whimsical notes.

"Bring your thoughts back to the days of your youth," instructed Sungazer. "Stop playing a moment and focus on the first time you ever saw a firefly."

Rona moved the flute away from her lips, and a slight smile curled her mouth.

"Good. Now try to feel the wonder or the awe that you felt."

"I felt sick," Rona confessed with a smirk. "I've been scared of bugs since I was a baby. I went crying for my mother."

"Afraid of a firefly?"

"I still run from flying bilgebugs."

Sungazer smiled.

"That's fine, then—recall the fear. Just paint the clearest picture that you can of the moment. Then, and only then, play your music so you can transform the fear into beauty.

"Fear kills the imagination. Recall the scent of the air that night and project it out. Hear the sounds of the firefly's wings fluttering and project that as well. See the bright yellow of its glow. Let's see that firefly appear in the dark before us. Remember the First Rule from your school days?"

"*If you can Imagine it, it has been and can be again.*" Rona recited.

Whim nodded, and after a moment, Rona put the instrument back to her lips and began to play.

The queen's eyes remained transfixed on the darkness. After a moment, they widened. A tiny splotch of light appeared out of nowhere, and it dipped and floated about, making small circles in the air.

"Good," Sungazer whispered. "Now make it —"

Before he could finish the sentence, the light was gone. Rona exhaled disgustedly.

"Sorry, Sungazer."

"No need to apologize. You did your best and got further than most," he said with a warm smile.

"Why don't you go back to your family?" Queen Chroma suggested. "Get a good night's sleep. We can try again tomorrow."

"Yes, Queen Chroma."

The queen ushered in a pair of palace guards. One was assigned to escort Rona safely back to the makeshift living quarters that had been set up in one of the many large halls of Everstood Castle.

The castle had been sealed to protect the people of Everstood from the wingers that hovered around the town. During the attack by Murkus's beasts, the main gates had been opened so they could take shelter there. Then darkness had fallen on the castle, on the glittering walls, striking fear into the hearts of those inside. So, although they appeared to be safe, they also felt trapped.

Queen Chroma paced the room.

"Still no sign or word from Pie O'Sky?"

"No," Sungazer said. "Last report was that he was taken by a filthy winger. What of the Stella Lumina?"

"We are far from certain that Rupert Starbright *is* the Stella Lumina. I just hope he is safe. He seems like such a sweet and decent boy."

"Where was he seen last?"

"I gave Weaver a direct order to protect him," Queen Chroma said with a frown.

"What's wrong?" Sungazer asked.

"Weaver has not been himself since Quix and Fancy were taken. Nor should he be. It is difficult for your heart to beat when it has been ripped from your chest," the queen said softly. "But he is strong."

"I know. But he seemed to be against using the boy for our needs. Was against it from the start."

"That's the parent in his soul."

"It does seem a terrible thing. Lure a child from his home to bring light to our dark days. I would die rather than see harm come to him."

"I imagine Weaver feels the same. Then again, if Rupert is the Stella Lumina…"

"If he is, then there is hope."

Murkus's groans and wails bounced around the stone halls that led from his lair. He exited his den and, with his body trembling, threw himself against the wall as if trying to stop the fit by knocking it out. His entire body was twitching and seemed to grow larger with each shudder and breath. He was going through some sort of change, and it sent waves of terrible pain through his body.

Slog stood nearby, his hands gently touching Murkus's back.

"Milord, you are growing stronge.! Yes!"

"Silence," Murkus mumbled. The giant stumbled to the opening in the wall and from it took the egg. He held it close to his face. "Yes, my child. For you, I do this. I will suffer this great change for you."

"You will be a perfect parent. A perfect dragon," Slog said with wide eyes.

"Bring me Xerks. I want to see those black moths of his Imagining," Murkus ordered as he pushed Slog towards the exit.

"I will leave you, milord. Getting the boy Xerks. Lovely black moths."

The heavy door slammed, and more groans and moans of pain exploded from within.

Not more than an hour later, a black cloud poured from an open window of Murkus's Keep—a swarm of black moths, each the size of the giant's own fist. Like coal dust in water they spread into the sky. Murkus's laughter roared around his castle, nor could Xerks's excitement at his Imagining be contained. The Darkledroons were airborne.

Chapter 13

A Quick and Fancy Tale

The lands just outside the wall were hard to walk on, especially compared to the much smoother grounds of The Garden of Dreams. The path was rocky and made bumpy and dangerous by the many roots and branches that crissed and crossed one's path. There were no roads, just difficult-to-follow trails. Luckily for Rupert, Weaver was the most expert tracker in all of Far-Myst.

Rupert hiked with his hands in his pockets and his shoulders hunched against the bitingly cold air. The sounds of strange plants and animals came from all around them. In the distance, the heavy footsteps of the stone folk could still be heard.

Weaver must have been very hungry, as his stomach was making sounds as loud as the creatures around them. As far as Rupert knew, he hadn't eaten a real meal in days. The thoughts of his children must have ruined his appetite.

His stomach growled again, this time loudly enough Rupert was startled.

"Was that your stomach making that sound?" he asked.

"Never mind. Just keep walking."

"Man, that sounded like my father snoring. I think you should eat something."

"I'm not hungry," Weaver snapped.

"Yes, you are. Your stomach just said so. At least eat some of the tree bark jerky."

Weaver ignored Rupert, but he knew the boy was right. He could feel his muscles weakening, his head getting light. He had to eat something, even though he felt, deep down, that he could not allow himself the luxury of food or rest. Still, a morsel would help.

Then he remembered that the pepper from the pepper poet plant Rupert had dropped was still in his pocket. His mouth watered as he thought about its spicy taste. Dream Weaver loved hot and spicy foods, and his mouth was famous all over Far-Myst for its ability to stand the hottest that chefs and plants had to offer.

He took out the pepper and popped it into his mouth. The heat from its juices flowed down his throat like liquid fire. The fruit of the pepper poet was rich in many vitamins and minerals. It would provide a boost of energy he needed. But the real treasure lay at its heart.

A story began to fill his head. A fable! Perhaps local gossip? Or news? Whatever it was, the words seemed to form in his memory as if he were remembering a long-forgotten tale. His eyes widened as the story took shape.

Could it be? As he played the words in his head, he grew more and more excited. He stopped in his tracks and smiled wide.

"They're alive!" he cried.

"Who?"

"My children."

Weaver's face seemed to lose ten years of age. For the first time since Rupert had met the man, he had a real smile on his face.

"The story. In the pepper," Weaver explained.

Rupert smiled.

"The plant said you might find this story interesting. Now I know what it meant. Said it was a 'quick and fancy tale.' I just figured he was bragging as usual." He yawned wide and stretched his arms high in the air.

"The story was told to the pepper poet by a small colorful bird of beautiful crystal feathers," Weaver continued. "A special bird, Imagined by a little girl. A little girl held prisoner. My little gem— my daughter Fancy."

"Where is she?"

"She's with her brother. In the Keep of Murkus. She's with all the other children of Far-Myst. They are being forced to work like slaves digging holes unless they agree to serve the fiend. But they are both fine."

"That's great. Did the story tell where the keep is?"

"No. They are in a place surrounded by clouds. Could be the Gnarled Hand Swamp or maybe as far as the Dreadful Hills in the Southern Feign region. No one has ever been able to locate Murkus's castle."

"But you know the most important thing. That they're alive and well," Rupert said through another yawn.

Weaver nodded, took a strip of jerky bark from his pack and bit into it. He took a mouthful of water from a bustle and looked with sympathy at Rupert.

"Why don't you let me carry you for a while. You can ride on my back," he offered.

"How much farther do we have to go before we can rest again?"

"I'd like to get as far as the Ruins of Elderwind. We should be safe there until sunrise. It's a good three-hour hike at steady pace."

Rupert took a deep breath and shook his head. "I'll walk."

"You sure, Dullz? You can ride on my back for a while. I feel like I suddenly have the strength of a herd of hilliphants."

"No, I can walk."

Rupert adjusted his jacket, but it could not keep out the growing chill. Weaver took his cloak off and wrapped it around Rupert's shoulders.

"Okay, but wear this. It will likely get even colder tonight."

"Thanks," Rupert said, tying the cloak tightly around his shoulders.

They continued on through the Wildness. Rupert's mind drifted as he followed the gardener along the dark, overgrown paths. They came upon a patch of moonlight berries that cast their light on the surroundings. Weaver broke off two bunches of the brightly glowing blue fruit to use as lanterns. They would glow for a couple of hours before their light faded away.

After another hour of hiking, a thin mist began to descend through the trees. The lights of the moonlight berries were fading. The wind picked up, and there was the distant sound of heavy rain washing down through the foliage. Soon, a heavy downpour soaked Rupert and Weaver to their skins. The voices of the night creatures had gone silent.

"Is there any place where we can dry off?" Rupert asked.

Weaver pointed toward a wide break in the trees. The sky far off was dark; only a slight glow of moonlight from behind the clouds made it visible at all. A tower of pure blackness stood against this dark-gray sky, a narrow band of shadow that rose up from the ground.

"Can you see the tower? Off on that hilltop?"

Rupert squinted then nodded.

"The Ruins of Elderwind. That's where we'll stay. We can make it there in an hour. Then I promise we will get the sleep we need."

When they finally came to the Ruins of Elderwind, the rain had eased a bit, but the wind had picked up. The spiraling tower of dark stone reached high above all the surrounding trees; the rain fell into Rupert's eyes as he peered up at it.

Weaver wasted no time, heading right for the entrance, once blocked by a steel gate that now lay rusted and rotted. The grounds around the tower were littered with large carved stones, broken slabs of what were once great walls, and oddly shaped masses of steel and marble.

"Come on, Dullz. Watch your step."

Rupert followed him through the doorway. The glow from the moonlight berries was just enough to see a few feet before them. A hallway led from the entrance and vanished into the darkness to the right. A staircase, narrow and steep, rose beside them. Weaver began climbing, holding the fading berries close to the steps.

"Shouldn't you use the Illuminor? Wouldn't that be brighter?" Rupert asked, climbing carefully behind.

"No."

They passed narrow windows at each landing. The tower smelled musty, and the scent of ancient incense and melted candles was still in the air. Rupert's legs were feeling like gooey wax themselves as he climbed up, up and up past ten more windows.

Finally, they stepped out onto an open room at the top of the tower that was partially covered with a crumbling overhang of roof. Positioned around the circular area were the remains of seven stone chairs. They all faced inward and stood on tall pedestals.

Weaver settled on the driest bit of floor he could find under an undamaged section of the roof and leaned against a marble column. Rupert took a peek out over the wall.

"How high up are we?"

"High. During the day you can see the castle as well as far, far off to the foothills of the Feigns."

"I was up even higher in Pie O'Sky's bagoon."

"Why don't you come out of the rain. You might dry off in a few hours. Wish I had some dry cloaks, but we'll have to make the best of what we have."

Rupert plopped down and made himself as comfortable as he could. The wind was blocked by the surrounding walls, and eventually, his shivering came under control.

They lay in silence for a while.

"What is this place?" Rupert asked finally.

"Long story."

"We're not going anywhere."

Weaver smiled. Rupert had a point.

"This is all that is left of the ancient Elderwind Castle. There was a time, many, many ages ago, when children didn't lose their Imaginings when they got older. Then, things got bad — greed, selfishness. People using their imaginations to do harm to others. The Elderwinds — also known as the Seven Figments — decided to limit the Imaginings to children who hadn't lost their innocence. These are their Seven Seats, where they would meet."

"You mean the pigs?" Rupert was confused.

"No." Weaver smiled again. "Those are the seven *Pigments*. The seven *Figments* help guide the Imagining energies." He looked around as memories filled his mind. "This place was once a beacon of the power of the Imagining. Even after Far-Myst split and it was abandoned and left to rot, it still sparked many peoples' imaginations."

Rupert was confused.

"What do you mean, split?"

"The Truseens, those who refused to give up the Imagining as adults, left Far-Myst and settled in the deepest Wildness, where some say they exist to this day. They were a strong-willed, thick-headed lot. But many say they were always true to their word. Would never abuse the power."

"Far-Myst is a lot more complicated than Graysland. No one ever splits off. We all pretty much live the same every day. Nothing really changes."

"Not always a bad thing, Dullz. But that was ages ago. Far-Myst has been a wonderful place to live, until recently. Anyway, this tower will always hold a special place in my heart."

"Why?"

Weaver closed his eyes.

"Get some sleep. We can talk more about this in the morning."

"First tell me why this place is so special."

Weaver gave him a hard look.

"Please."

Weaver's face softened, and he gathered his thoughts.

"I came up here one crystal-clear night with someone very special. The sky was packed with stars. There was a wonderful cool breeze. It was that night I asked Celestia to marry me. I always feel safe here. I've come here every year since she left me."

"Where did she go?" Rupert asked innocently.

"Passed on."

"How?"

"Let's get some sleep, Dullz. I want to get back on the road at sunrise."

Rupert nodded and thought it best not to ask any more questions.

"I'll try. I'm really tired, but my mind is wide awake," he said with a yawn.

"You've been through a lot in the last two days. Natural for your mind to spin."

The wind was howling up the staircase. The sound of the rain piddling into the puddles that were scattered about seemed oddly comforting to Rupert, now that he was out of its reach. Weaver was right. He had been through more in the last two days than he had in his entire life in Graysland.

He wondered what his parents were thinking. Surely, Squeem what have told them about Pie O'Sky's door. Rupert wondered if his father had been right. Should he have stayed away from the colorful man who came to Graysland in his strange balloon? After all, Pie O'Sky had not been completely honest about the situation in Far-Myst.

He wondered then if he would ever get back. Did he want to go back? As uncomfortable and tired as he was, this was definitely more exciting than raking leaves or sitting in boring Mrs. Drumpsitter's class. What about Grandma Folka? Would Weaver's friend in Flowseen really have a cure? What if she didn't? Would this entire ordeal have been a waste of time?

And what of his ability to help Far-Myst, that Pie O'Sky and Queen Chroma had spoken of? If he could be of help, why did Weaver want to send him home? He felt his spinning thoughts drift away, and he finally fell asleep.

Rupert awoke a couple of hours later. His entire body was shaking. He was cold. It was still raining, not with the big drops like before but a thick misty kind of rain that soaked everything it touched. He wished he could be dry. Warm. Maybe then he could really relax. Perhaps he could make a fire. But how? The camper grass needed to be bone-dry to ignite.

Why? he wondered. *Why can't fire get wet? Why can't there be a special kind of fire that can still burn in the rain? Wouldn't that make more sense?* If a fish could fly and open doors why not a fire that could burn in the rain?

Rupert's thoughts went to the Child's Eye Museum and all of its wonders. He was certain somewhere amongst all the strange objects was a device to make a fire that could burn in the rain. Or maybe even under water. And if there wasn't, surely, in a place where the imagination was so powerful, it could be done.

He tried to see such a fire in his mind. Would it be yellow or orange or red like normal fire? He wondered. Maybe it would be bright blue. Maybe it would smell like burnt sugar. It could turn the raindrops into many-colored fireflies!

Rupert's eyes were closed, and he could feel sleep coming back. His thoughts became dreamy, and in his mind, the blue fire that smelled like caramel was burning. It was a beautiful fire—he could almost feel its warmth and smell its sweet aroma. The brightness of the fire danced in his eyes. He felt dry and warm.

"Dullz!" Weaver shouted.

Rupert's eyes snapped open, and he gasped. Before him was a campfire, burning bright blue and sending the scent of burnt sugar to his nose. The rain fell on it, and each wet drop transformed into a colorful blinking firefly and flew off into the night.

"I did it!" he said excitedly.

"You did what?" Weaver sounded as if he was almost afraid to ask.

"I imagined that fire!"

Weaver studied him with amazement. He looked into the blue flames that flickered and warmed them.

"Rupert, how did you do this?"

"I don't know. I just thought about it."

"It's not possible."

"I thought everything was possible in Far-Myst."

"For the children of *Far-Myst*. Not for the ones from Graysland or anywhere else."

"Maybe Pie O'Sky was right."

"Put it out."

"But why? We're freezing. This'll help dry our clothes."

"Just do it!"

"How? Water won't work. I imagined a fire that was waterproof."

"Murkus might see this. It could give away our location."

"Maybe I can imagine a way to put it out."

"No! Enough Imaginings out of you. It's not a toy to play with. Can be very dangerous to someone who doesn't know how to handle it."

Rupert didn't know what to do. As Weaver paced, he took advantage of the warmth. He didn't care if Murkus saw it—it felt wonderful to be warm again.

And it was very exciting. Not only had he used an imagination he never knew he had to open a door to a place he had never heard of, he had made blue fire appear out of nothing. There it was, a thought from his mind, sitting before him as real as the rain.

Then something very unexpected happened. The seven ancient stone chairs began to glow brighter and brighter as colored lights descended from the sky and bathed each seat. Seven odd figures appeared. Weaver's eyes grew wide. Rupert smiled.

"What the heck is happening, Mr. Weaver?"

"The Figments! They've returned," Weaver gasped.

They were all a head shorter than Rupert and had large, round heads. Large eyes, tiny noses and tiny ears filled out their faces. Three were female and three were male. The seventh was no more than a misty shadow.

"They look like giant babies," Rupert commented under his breath.

Weaver shot him a look of shock.

"Rupert! Shhh!"

One of the colored beams of light brightened to pure white.

"Hello, Rupert Starbright," said the Figment. "My name is Dazzler, and I handle the figment of vision. It is I who allows that fire to burn with such a rich color."

"Hello, Mr. Dazzler."

The next chair was engulfed in the pure white beam of light. This Figment was coated in a patchwork of pink fuzzy fur, silver and gold scales, blue glass, yellow skin, green feathers, red leather, white rubber, orange wood, purple paper and indigo metal.

"Rupert Starbright," the Being greeted him. "I am Feltser. I watch over the figment of touch. Pie O'Sky believes you may be the Stella Lumina. Are you?"

Rupert shrugged. "I don't know."

"If I may say…" Weaver stepped forward. "This boy was a guest of Queen Chroma's. He is from a place called Graysland. I am seeing him to Flowseen to get him back home. It's become too dangerous for him here."

"Dangerous? Nonsense! Not for a boy with his ability."

"We are not really sure of his ability," Weaver warned.

"Did he not produce that fire with his imagination? Here, atop the Tower of Elderwind?"

"Yep! I sure did. Shocked the poop out of me, I must admit," Rupert bragged in great excitement.

"The ancient text tells of a child who comes to Far-Myst from another land. We sensed his ability the moment the first blue flame flickered. I, naturally, realized the heated silk of the fire's surface."

Five more lights illuminated five more Figments. One by one, they introduced themselves.

"I am Formi," said a being whose shape constantly changed. "Shape is my game. Through me, those flickering flames can so easily morph their form."

The next Figment vibrated with all sorts of sounds—buzzes and beeps, pops and gargles, wooshes and slams, soft chimes and sharp whistles. He spoke through his symphony of sounds.

"My name is Tenor. Sound is my art. Listen to my work in the crackling of that fire."

126

The next was surrounded by colorful mists of multi-colored smoke. Rupert's nose twitched as an endless variety of smells from flower-blossom lovely to dripsludge-stinky wafted to it.

"I'm Essence. If it smells, it's my figment. My power wafts in the sweetness of those blue flames."

The next was dressed in chain mail armor that glittered with a thousand colors.

"I'm known as Venture. You can't imagine an adventure without me. Hidden within those flames are infinite tales about infinite paths you will choose from, young Starbright."

The seventh Figment was the ghost-like floating mass like colorful tissue paper shimmying in a breeze. Billions of tiny, tiny stars glowed deep inside it. It didn't say a word. Rupert, expecting an introduction, stood silent for a moment.

"Who are you?" he braved.

"That is Tangle," Venture explained. "She deals with all the things yet to be imagined. Yet to be thought. Yet to be dreamed. She is the fire yet to burn. The road yet to be paved. The fruit yet to be born from a flower yet to bloom."

Rupert felt like his brain had been dipped in honey and was being nibbled on by many, many butterflies. It tickled!

"But it is *you* we must discuss, not us. We must see the strength of your powers," Essence insisted. "We have dreamed of having our abilities challenged by the Stella Lumina."

"If you are the one," Formi added, stroking his ever-changing chin.

"I am not sure he has such powers," Weaver argued.

"I made this blue fire appear," Rupert bragged again.

There was suddenly a great discussion among the Seven Figments. Chitter and chatter and yipping and yapping, smells and sounds, shapes and colors of every imaginable kind filled the air. Finally, they quieted down and turned their attention back to Rupert.

"Would you please imagine something else?" Formi requested.

"Something that smells like fresh coggleberries?" added Essence.

"And sings like a kriffin fish?" Tenor added.

Once again the chitter and chatter of the Figments erupted, each tossing suggestions and ideas for the boy to Imagine.

Weaver rolled his eyes and interrupted.

"With all due respect..." He stepped forward. "I must get this boy home. His parents must be worried sick by now, and I refuse to inflict that sort of pain on anyone."

"Not a wise idea, Sir Weaver," Venture said. "If Rupert is the Stella Lumina then he is destined to help Far-Myst and our troubles."

"So, what am I to do?"

"What did Queen Chroma ask you to do?" Formi asked.

"She ordered me to protect him."

"Did she ever order you to take him home?"

"No."

"Then why are you, a member of the Twelve, disobeying an order?"

"I'm not. Getting him home is the best protection I can offer."

"Queen Chroma is a just and honorable leader. She would never intentionally order someone to cause harm to anyone else. I suggest—and all my fellow figments agree—that you continue to protect Starbright from Murkus and his flying denizens. Take him to Flowseen, as you planned."

Weaver seemed confused

"But you just said…"

"Your paths are linked. If Starbright is, in fact, the Stella Lumina, his journey home will first take him on the back roads of Far-Myst's history. Am I not right, Tangle?"

All eyes turned to the ghostly form. She did not reply with so much as a nod.

"It's inevitable," Feltzer added.

"Probably," corrected Venture.

Weaver swallowed and took a deep breath.

"Fine. Then I will continue to escort Rupert to Flowseen so he can get home. If the Fates of Imagination or the Figments want to intervene, so be it."

"We do not intervene in anything, Sir Weaver. We only allow what is properly Imagined to be," Formi explained. "Imagine well, Mr. Starbright."

With that, the Seven Figments vanished in brightening lights. After a moment, all went dark but for the dancing blue flames.

Weaver took a deep breath and looked to Rupert.

"Get some more sleep. We'll talk about this in the morning."

"They think I am the one who will help Far-Myst, don't they? Even if I try to go home, something is going to happen to keep me here."

Weaver shrugged. "I guess we'll see, won't we?"

Rupert shrugged, too, rested his head back on the ground and fell asleep instantly, enjoying the warmth of his fire in his dreams.

Chapter 14

Darkledroons!

Slog paced outside the den of Murkus like an expecting father. Terrible moans and groans leaked out from under the heavy wooden door.

"My poor lord. Poor, poor lord!" he mumbled. "A terrible ordeal. Terrible but utterly natural. Wonderful! What a wonderful thing for my lord to go through."

He continued to mumble and pace, smile and frown. He dropped his head in utter despair then would suddenly dance in complete joy. Something strange was happening to Murkus. It was awesome and powerful and dreadfully frightening.

A shadowy form suddenly appeared at the end of the corridor, warped by the light of the torches positioned along the walls. A flock of Darkledroons approached. They came to an obedient halt before Slog, who looked at them with great suspicion.

"What is it? Why do you come to disturb your master?"

The black moths dipped and dived and flew in small, tight circles.

"Trying to tell me something? A secret? A tale? Then get on with it! The lord is busy."

Suddenly, the door to Murkus's lair flew open. Slog turned and recoiled in fear.

"What is going on?" Murkus growled softly.

"My...my lord, don't you look wonderful! Yes! Yes, a natural change!"

Murkus stepped out of the darkened lair. He was, indeed, changed. His skin, although still the moist-worm color, was covered in scales. His head was larger and more elongated. His hands were like those of some spiny lizard. His feet had morphed into large, webbed pads with hooked talons instead of toes. A tail whipped angrily behind him. His eyes were fiery orange.

"Why are the Darkledroons here? Do they have news to report?"

"I was just about to ask that very question, milord!" Slog said, backing off some more.

Murkus pushed him aside and turned to the hovering mass of creatures.

"The child? Is there news?"

The swarm reshaped itself into a flat, square wall. A flickering light sparked on the surface, and an image appeared. A small blue campfire, seen from on high. The image grew until the sleeping forms of Rupert and Weaver were clearly seen.

Murkus's expression tightened, and his eyes grew wide.

"Very clever, young Xerks," he whispered to himself, impressed by the Darkledroons. He studied the image of the blue fire. "So, this boy from afar does have power. A fire of pure Imagining atop the Tower of the Elderwinds!" He turned to Slog. "Get me Quix and Xerks!"

Slog backed off slowly, nodding and bowing.

Murkus had no time to be nice.

"Now!"

From the depths of his throat came a blast of red flames that singed Slog's bottom as he ran down the hall. Smoke wafted from Murkus's nostrils as his mind formed awful thoughts reflected on his face—a face growing more and more dragon-like.

He turned to the moths.

"Go, rejoin the others! We must weaken the boy's abilities for now. Strike fear into him. Fear kills the imagination. Keep him frightened and weak until I can take advantage of his Imaginings. Do what you wish to the gardener!"

The swarm flew off with purpose.

⚙

The sun peeked over the wall of the tower like a peeping clown. Bright red with a yellow haze, it was smiling at the beautiful morning and nudged Rupert's eyes open.

He didn't see anything so great about the morning. In fact, he wished he could wallop the sun in its glowing, hot face for waking him up. He threw his arm over his eyes. It helped block the light, but there was something else poking him awake. Sound filling his ears. Birds. Lots of birds, singing and tweeting and twilling.

"Shut up," he mumbled, "I'm still tired."

"Rupert, get up."

Rats, Weaver's awake. Rupert opened one eye. The brilliance of the blue sky was blinding. He opened the other, and slowly, they adjusted. Weaver was checking the supplies in his pack. He looked like he was ready to hit the road again. There would be no rolling over for an extra snooze this morning.

"Time to get to your feet, Mr. Dullz. There are roads to meet and feet to be worn out."

Rupert surrendered and got up, joining Weaver beside one of the Seven Seats.

"I hope you got enough sleep. Here, eat this." Weaver handed him a hunk of dried fruit and a water bustle. "Take a look at the view — you'll see its better than it was last night," he said, taking a drink from a bustle.

Rupert went to the edge of the wall as if he were carrying an elephant on his back. He was perked up by the view. A carpet of many-colored trees spread out in all directions, dipping and rising on meandering hills. He filled his lungs with the clean, sweet-smelling air.

The smile that was forming on his face vanished, though, when he looked north. Everstood Castle was much closer than he had imagined. He felt as if he had walked a million miles and had expected it to be a mere dot on the horizon. Yet there it stood, close enough for him to see the beautiful brickwork on its towers.

But it was not its closeness that made him frown. It was the color — or rather, lack of color — that did. It was no longer the marvelous site he had seem from Pie O'Sky's bagoon. It looked like a huge paving stone of the kind that lined the streets of Graysland. A mere shadow against a blue sky. Gone were the million billion tiny jewels that had captured his imagination when he'd first laid eyes on it.

He shivered. Although the sun was warm on his skin, there was still that chill in the air, blowing in from the south. He walked across the courtyard and peered out to that horizon. His eyes widened.

"Those ugly black clouds look closer," he said.

"That's because they are. They'll bring the ugliness of Murkus, I imagine." Weaver sounded sad as he lifted the pack and threw it over his shoulder.

"How far are we gonna walk today," Rupert asked, lifting his own pack.

"We should be able to get across the Frothing River and spend the night in Story — it's a tiny village. We will be safe there. We can stay at a friend's house. A fellow Illuminorian."

"You have friends everywhere, don't you?" Rupert noted with a smile.

Weaver nodded and walked to the stairway. Rupert took the fortune seed from his pocket and studied its bright-red sheen for a moment. *What sort of difficulties lie ahead?* he wondered.

He had no time for such concerns. He was about to put it back into his pocket when he felt a stab of heat on his palm. He looked at the seed. It was glowing brighter! It felt warm.

Suddenly, the sunlight went dark, just for a moment. Rupert looked skyward. For a split second, he thought it was one of the flying holes he had seen with Pie O'Sky, but this was different. It was a cloud of small black flying creatures.

"Mr. Weaver! Look!"

Weaver followed Rupert's line of sight skyward, and his face went white.

"Downstairs, Rupert!"

"What are they?"

"I haven't a clue, but the fortune seed is glowing. They are a force of Dark Imaginings."

He drew his Illuminor, grabbed Rupert's arm and hurried him into the stairwell. The swarm of Darkledroons descended.

Rupert and Weaver had only gone down a single flight when the air popped and cracked above them.

"They're in!" cried Rupert.

"Just keep moving, lad! Don't let them touch you!"

He kept Rupert ahead of him and held the Illuminor high. The Darkledroons were gaining rapidly. Rupert tried to ignore the growing noise, a sound just like piles of dried leaves being sucked into a leaf-collecting truck.

Down and around they ran on the ancient stone steps until they hit ground level. The light of the entrance was before them, and Rupert bee-lined toward it. He didn't see what Weaver saw.

"Dullz!"

The devious Darkledroons had split their attack on the tower, and a part of the swarm had flown down to its base. They hovered just outside the doorway, waiting to pounce.

Rupert stopped and turned to Weaver.

"Where can we go?"

Weaver launched himself in front of Rupert and swiped the illuminated dagger into the cloud of black moths. The light of pure imagination dissolved many into nothingness and scattered the rest.

"Straight ahead! Back into the forest!" Weaver ordered, spinning to face the other swarm. "Run as fast as you can!"

Rupert put his head down and raced across the rubble-strewn land as Weaver slashed at the onslaught of moths. He fought desperately to keep them at bay, but a number of the horrid winged shadows slipped past the brilliant light of the Illuminor and landed blows, dissolving into his body wherever they contacted bare skin.

Weaver began to feel queasy and sick. It was not the kind of nausea one might get from eating too many lemon cookies and hot peppers. This was a terrible uneasiness. An uncontrollable sensation of soon-to-come doom. That was the Darkledroons' weapon. They dampened and darkened the spirit. They injected fear into the blood.

He fought against the ugly feelings creeping from his gut into his mind, but he had a more threatening battle at hand. The Darkledroons were getting bolder, and with each swing of the Illuminor, ten of the attackers would slip through. Weaver tried to retreat and stumbled over a hunk of marble. He went down, and the Illuminor flew from his hand.

Rupert felt like he had a croaking bullfrog in his mouth his heart was beating so hard. He leaped and jumped around and over the rubble, his eyes fixed on the tree line and the uncertain darkness that lay beyond it. His mind was in overdrive.

An umbrella – if I only had an umbrella. How about an umbrella that gave off light like the Illuminor? Yeah, that would work. Can I do it? Can I imagine such a thing like I did the fish key or the blue waterproof fire?

He tried to get an image in his head of such a shield. Only flashes of his father's tattered black bumbershoot popped into his mind.

No good! He scolded himself. *That dumb thing can't even block raindrops!*

Rupert's legs were taken from under him as he tripped over the bent steel of the fallen gate. He landed with a painful thud on the moist, rocky ground and glanced over his shoulder. The swarm of Darkledroons was all over Weaver. The gardener was almost buried in black, and the Illuminor's light was gone.

He scanned the grounds. The Illuminor lay on the ground amidst the rubble, far from Weaver's grasp. Rupert raced to the device and dared to take it into his own hands.

Weaver was losing the battle. One after another, the moths struck him. He rolled on the ground, trying desperately to cover any exposed skin. Rupert raised the Illuminor into the air as colorful light sprang from it like a water fountain.

"Hey! Stop it! Leave him alone!"

The Darkledroons froze. Then, to Rupert's dismay, they poured off Weaver and took to the air, coming his way. He panicked and raced off, the cloud of living black horror close behind.

The first few seeped into his eyeballs. Like mud being tossed at him, the splotches of black struck his face, his hands and his arms.

"Get off me! Go away!"

The glow of the Illuminor faded fast as fear took hold of Rupert's heart. He was filled with dark thoughts. The sound of his Grandma Folka's terrible hacking cough filled his mind. His parents were sobbing and searching all of Graysland for their vanished son. Squeem, jealous that Rupert had gone through the door without him, was smashing the door to bits with his rake. Nightwingers surrounded him and mocked him. Dark pits of burning leaves threatened to engulf him. Rupert was lost in a dark, lonely forest of his own mind.

The shadows were all around him, and they never stopped their attack. The fish key, the blue fire and the protective umbrella of many colors were a far, far memory, lost in a maze of fear and anger. He felt his body rise then drop into a sea of dripsludge. He felt like his mouth was corked with stones. He wanted to scream out the terror that filled his heart, but he could not breathe.

"Rupert," came a voice in the dark, "open your eyes."

He gasped as his eyes flew open.

"It's okay. Them bloody things are gone."

Rupert was confused. He looked around and saw he was in the forest under a canopy of twisting, ropy branches that created a cathedral-like ceiling of leaf-green and bark-brown. Dream Weaver sat beside him, wiping a wet cloth over his forehead.

His entire body was trembling, and his gaze darted about as he waited for an attack any moment. He could not stop the shivering that shook every muscle in his body.

"My parents, my grandmother—they're dead," he muttered.

"They're fine. That's just the dark lies of those moths," Weaver tried to explain.

Rupert didn't believe him. He jumped to his feet and raced around as if looking for something.

"Dullz! Relax. Everything will be fine."

"Wingers—there are wingers in the trees!" Rupert pointed wildly up at the shadowy pockets in the treetops.

"No wingers around here, boy. Not a one," Weaver said softly.

Rupert continued to search all around him. His legs shook. Weaver put a hand on his shoulder, and he jumped.

"It's all in your mind. Give it time. It will clear."

He rubbed his eyes then looked around the pine needle-covered ground.

"You lost it," he whispered to himself. "It fell from your hands."

Weaver frowned.

"I had your Illuminor. I lost it."

"I have it." Weaver tapped the dagger that hung on his belt.

"I tried to use it. I tried to chase them away."

"I should whack your bum for such a stunt. You shouldn't toy with what you don't know."

"You were being killed," Rupert mumbled, digging through his muddy memories.

"I wasn't being killed. I was trying to keep them from you. Give you a chance to get away."

"You dropped it. I had to do something."

An expression of embarrassment and anger tightened Weaver's face.

"You should not have touched it. No child should touch such a thing unless they have earned that right."

Rupert's mind was still spinning. The thoughts in his head were like leaves caught in a spiraling gust of wind.

"My grandma. She's sick. She's gonna die if I don't help her."

"Ignore those thoughts."

"My parents. Squeem. They're mad at me."

Weaver's face softened a bit.

"We should be going. It's a healthy hike to Story. The walking'll do your mind good."

Rupert nodded and took his pack. They headed off into the depths of the woods.

They walked in silence on the soft carpet of pine needles and the last years' autumn leaf-fall. The morning birds that had awakened Rupert were silent, perhaps frightened by the arrival of the Darkledroons. His mind was still abuzz with thoughts of his grandmother, his parents and Squeem. He missed Squeem. He wondered how Squeem would have reacted to all the amazing things he had seen and experienced during the last few days.

Squeem was a shy boy who tended to choose less rocky paths in life, but he was also a loyal and considerate friend. Surely, if Rupert had risked his own life to save *him* from a swarm of nightmarish moths, Squeem would have appreciated the effort.

141

He would have thanked him for the act of friendship. Rupert was certain Squeem would not have scolded him.

He looked up at Weaver, a few steps ahead, and studied the man's hard face.

He's still worried about his kids.

But there was something else. From the moment, Rupert met Dream Weaver, he had felt he was an unwanted burden. Weaver had said so himself. He could be helping Queen Chroma, or attempting to rescue his children if he hadn't been ordered to protect a boy from a strange land. He knew Weaver wanted him back home and away from the troubles of Far-Myst.

And what of this talk of the Stella Lumina? Rupert was not really sure what it all meant. How could he, the child of a doctor's assistant and a coffin-maker, who lived in a boring home on a boring street in a boring land, be the answer to the troubles of the most unboring place Rupert had ever been to?

Then again, he *had* created a waterproof fire using his imagination. Could he do it again? Could he create a cure for his grandmother and take it back with him to Graysland?

He gathered his thoughts the best he could but had no clue where to begin. To imagine a cure, he had to understand what caused the coffus. He didn't know about such things.

The wind picked up and, for a moment, cooled the warm sun that fell through the mesh of trees and made bright-yellow puddles on the ground. He felt a sudden vibration under his feet. It felt just like his mattress did when a leaf truck drove by his bedroom window.

"What's that?" he asked.

"It's the waterfall trees getting replenished. The water from the Frothing River moves through their root systems underground."

"You mean the trees way back in the garden?"

"Those and others in the area. Waterfall trees have the longest and most complex root structures of any tree in Far-Myst. They're like great pipes."

The rumble and muffled whoosh continued for a few minutes until finally fading off in the distance. For a while, only their soft footsteps broke the silence.

"What happened to the birds?" Rupert wondered as he searched the treetops for a sign of wing or feather. "They get scared off by those black things?"

"I don't know. Maybe you should ask the birds?"

Jeez, Rupert thought. *What a grump. Somebody got up on the wrong side of the campfire.*

Weaver stopped. All his senses seem to go into action. He sniffed the air and cocked his head to hear better.

"What's wrong?" Rupert was afraid to know.

Slowly, Weaver turned his head. Rupert knew they were in trouble by the way his eyebrows rose. Something horrible was behind them.

"Rupert," Weaver whispered, "on my count of three, run. And stay close. There's a place where we'll be safe."

Rupert swallowed and nodded. He couldn't resist. He turned around.

A huge black skull hovered a few feet above the forest floor. He could see, even from this distance, that it wasn't solid, as it flickered and wavered in the air. Darkledroons, a lot of them, gathered into a horrid shape, floating closer and closer.

"One...two..." Weaver whispered,"...three. Now!"

Chapter 15

The Water Way

They took off on the cleared path. The skull exploded into its individual terrors and, in a black flood, washed towards them. Weaver was running fast, and Rupert pushed his body to new limits to keep up with him.

They veered off the friendly path and into the thick brush that lined it. Rupert was afraid to turn around, but he could sense that the Darkledroons were closing in. Terror bubbled in his stomach; the seeds of fear that had been planted there in the last attack was far too fresh. It was not an experience he cared to go through again. He was sure Weaver shared that same fear.

The wispy branches of bushes and tall plants whipped him across his face. They stung like mosquitoes but he didn't care. He felt the ground beneath his feet tilt down, and soon he was struggling to stay upright as small rocks slipped free from the loose soil beneath him. Up ahead, he could see a tremendous black boulder, and surrounding it was a net of roots. Weaver headed directly toward it.

Rupert squinted. Was it a rock? No, it was a dark opening. A cave.

There was a tickle at his ear. From the corner of his eye, he saw two of the fearsome moths. He picked up his pace with every ounce of energy he could muster. The sickening feeling, like a cold, wet finger, entered his ear. In his mind, Rupert saw a coffin. A black box. He heard his grandmother cough…

The cave opening was mere feet away. He would ignore the nasty feelings. He would outrun the beasts. But wouldn't they simply follow them in? What good would it do to hide in a dark cave?

He had no choice but to trust Weaver.

Weaver disappeared into the opening, and Rupert followed. As if hitting a wall, the swarm of Darkledroons halted at the mouth of the cave. The few who dared to enter dissolved into nothingness, like tissue paper in water.

To Rupert's surprise, the cave was not a cave at all. He stared down a long, long circular passage of tightly braided roots. The walls were aglow with a red gooey substance that leaked from open pores that dotted the surface of the roots.

Weaver ran in a few yards then drew his Illuminor and waited.

"As I hoped, they were too scared to follow. Too much imagination energy in here," he whispered.

"What is this place?"

"Shh!" Weaver ordered. "Keep your voice down. We have to be careful. Don't want the humdrummers giving us trouble."

"The what?"

"These are root systems, called *runs*. Humdrummers keep them clear of obstructions. Water runs through these tubeways from the Frothing River to all the stands of waterfall pines in the region. That glowing red sap—that's what the humdrummers eat. So, we can't dawdle. We don't want to be mistaken for a blockage by the drummers, and we certainly don't want to be around when the water flows."

"How often does the water flow?"

"Hard to say what nature's needs are. Just stay close, as always. If a humdrummer approaches, flatten yourself against the wall. They won't eat you or anything nasty like that, but they'll try to push you out of the runs. They can be very persistent. Could break your crazy bone or something if they send you flying."

Rupert nodded and looked down the stretch of the runs. The glowing red juice lit the way as far as his eyes could see.

They began a fast-paced trek through the runs. The tubes smelled of pine needles and fresh rain, and everything was moist to the touch. Rupert wiped some of the glowing sap off on his fingers and sniffed it. Its smell was powerful—it cleared his nose and made his eyes water.

"That stuff will clear the toughest nose weasels from your nostrils," said Weaver.

Rupert smiled and wiped the sap onto his pant leg, and they continued.

When they came to double and triple forks where tubes split off and ran to different places, Weaver would stop and listen, tilting his head towards each branch.

"You listening for the humdrummers?" Rupert asked.

"No. You'll know it when they come. I'm listening for sounds of the Frothing. Water makes a loop in the runs—what isn't drained off by the trees is sent back to the river. We want to come out close to the river but not too close, if you get my meaning."

They traveled for nearly to an hour before a strange sound bounded through the tubes.

Hummm Hummm! Boom boom boom!

"There's one of the buggers," whispered Weaver, quietly moving Rupert out of the creature's line of sight.

Rupert wasn't sure if he wanted to laugh at the sight of the odd creature or run for his life.

It looked like a giant bullfrog, but where a head should be there was a flat surface, like the tightly pulled skin of a drumhead. Atop that was a single eyeball the size of his Mom's hair bun. The creature hopped forward on powerful legs and stared dead ahead, and the *Hummm! Hummm!* sounded. Then the flat drum of its head pounded, as if an inner fist was punching the surface from inside. With each punch, the sheet of skin protruded outward with a deep *Boom! Boom!*

Weaver leaned closer to Rupert and whispered, "They have nothing in the way of side vision, but if they spot you, they'll wallop ya! Watch."

He took a piece of jerky bark from his pocket and tossed it in front of the creature. With lightning speed, the humdrummer stretched the drum skin more than ten feet with its bizarre, fist-like protrusion. The fleshy punch struck only air, but made very clear to Rupert the dangers of getting too close.

"Wow, that's bizarre," he whispered.

"That could knock you for a loop. They just want to be left alone to lick the red juice. In return for their meals, they keep the runs clear. A great example of give-and-take in Far-Myst's natural world."

"It's coming towards us!"

"Don't worry. Just stay pressed up against the wall. She'll pass."

Rupert obeyed, flattening himself as much as he could against the braided roots that made up the wall. He could feel the leaking red juice seeping into his clothing and sticking on the bare skin of his arms. It fell oddly cool.

The humdrummer hopped closer, stopping to let its eye take in the view. It hopped again, this time landing with a thud inches from Rupert and Weaver. Rupert didn't even breathe.

"Notice the way the drum skin vibrates?" Weaver pointed out in a whisper.

Rupert refused to reply. He tipped his head in a barely recognizable nod. Weaver smiled.

"It's okay. She doesn't see us as a threat," Weaver assured him. "Otherwise, her drum would be pounding."

"Okay."

A long, ribbon-like tongue shot from a small opening on the drum face and began licking the red juice from the wall, moving closer to Rupert. His face contorted in disgust as the sticky wet tongue swept across his cheeks and nose. Weaver smiled wide.

"Yuck," Rupert mumbled, wiping his face with his sleeve.

"Don't be so quick to judge," Weaver said with a smile. "The spit of a drummer can do wonders for cuts and nicks. Very medicinal."

Suddenly, his smile fell off his face, and his eyes bulged. A half-dozen humdrummers were bounding their way! He grabbed Rupert by the shoulder and pushed him back in the direction they had come.

"Quick, Rupert! Something's up!"

A deep drumming boomed, and the fleshy fist shot from the leading humdrummer and struck Weaver square in the back. He stumbled but managed to keep his balance. The humming and drumming grew louder as the herd grew more excited. Another fleshy fist struck, this time smacking Rupert in his tush and throwing him off his feet and onto the ground. He felt a breeze as a humdrummer hopped over him.

He was trying to get to his feet when another one struck. Rupert tumbled across the ground and into Weaver. Weaver grabbed his hand and dragged him down a side tube but stopped again. Three more drummers were coming that way!

"This way." Weaver took the other fork. Another humdrummer fist struck and knocked him to the ground. Rupert turned just in time to see the next blow coming and managed to leap to the wall of the tube and escape being struck.

The humdrummer hopped past. He helped Weaver up.

"Where are they going?" he asked in a panic.

"They're fleeing."

"Fleeing what?"

Weaver looked sick. "Just follow me, lad and—"

He ducked another blow and flattened himself on the ground as the humdrummer leaped over his huddled body. He got back up and looked at Rupert, still standing flush against the wall. The humming and the drumming were fading.

"What are they running from?" Rupert asked again.

"That," Weaver said flatly.

Then Rupert heard it—a rushing sound that grew louder and louder. It sounded like one of the freight trains he heard howling in the quiet Graysland nights.

Weaver rushed forward and grabbed him in a bear hug.

"Put your arms around my waist and hold on tighter than you ever hugged your grandma, lad!"

Rupert did as he was told. Then he saw it coming—a wall of water that filled the passage from floor to ceiling.

"Take a deep breath and hold it!"

Just as Rupert filled his lungs with air the huge wave struck. They were carried through the runs on a freight train of water from the Frothing River. It hit so fast and so completely engulfed them that it took him a moment to get over the shock of the cold.

Rupert opened his eyes and could only see white foam bubbling around them. They were bounced off the walls as they were flushed around turns into forks in the path.

The strangest and most unexpected sight was watching, through the wash of murky water and bubbles, various root-ways closing off, and they were rerouted as valves of interwoven roots sealed them off. It was as if some larger mind was working it all.

Rupert held tight and wondered where they would come out. Although it had only been a few seconds, he felt they had been moving for an hour. He was trying not to think about his breath. How long could he hold it? Would they travel all the way back to the Garden of Dreams and have to start their journey all over?

And what about the river? What happened if they were spat out directly into the Frothing River? Rupert was not a swimmer. He wasn't even sure he could float. He wished they were on a boat, like the ones the workmen used back in Graysland on the West River to fish or clear the leaves that would often clog the sewage outputs.

His lungs ached for air. He wanted to breathe. He wanted desperately to open his mouth and take a deep breath of the wonderfully fresh air of Far-Myst. He couldn't, of course, so he thought about boats again. He wondered what a boat in Far-Myst would look like.

Any way you wanted! he figured.

Maybe the boat would move by its own power. You could just lie back, and the boat would be smart enough to take you wherever you asked it to. It could be shaped like a hippopotamus…

Yes—a *hippoboatamus*! It might even be bright yellow with a large blue umbrella covering it in case it rained or the sun was too hot. It would have four—no, six—webbed feet that would send it at fast but comfortable speeds along any river then let it walk up on shore so the passengers would not get their feet wet.

Rupert could see the yellow hippoboatamus with the blue umbrella clearly in his mind. It helped him forget about his lungs and burning eyes and the freezing water.

The blackness of the tubes was broken only by splotches of glowing red sap that streaked by like blood-red lightning flashes. How much farther? He could hear the valves opening and closing, and feel the wash of foamy bubbles.

Then he felt a tug on his belt. Weaver gestured ahead with a quick nod. There was sunlight at the distant end of the root-way. An opening to the outside! Like golden honey, the shafts of sun poured in from somewhere above.

Rupert felt panic. He was so close yet so far. Could he hold his breath for ten more seconds?

It was as if suddenly the world went into slow motion and the water had turned to mud. Rupert closed his eyes. He swallowed a few drops of water that leaked into his mouth. It was cold and tasted like pine needles. He shivered, and when he opened his eyes, his heart skipped a beat. The exit was sealing up with a valve of tightly woven roots! A few more feet...and a few more seconds...

Weaver shifted around and moved Rupert in front so he would get out first. The valve was half-way shut, and the world around them was darkening again. A couple of more feet. More water flowed into Rupert's mouth. There was a great rush of bubbly water, air and sunlight.

The warm air hit Rupert like a hug. He was still floating in the water, but his head was above the surface. He gasped, spat the water from his mouth and tried to fill his lungs. It took a few attempts, and when he did he wanted to shout out in joy.

Until he realized he was alone.

He looked around frantically. He was in a wide river. The mighty Frothing! On either shore was thick vegetation. He could see where he had washed out of the runs. Water was still bubbling from it as the valve continued to close. But Weaver was nowhere in sight.

The current was strong, and Rupert was at its mercy. His head went under, and he got another mouthful of water. He forced his head above the surface and spat. He was scared again.

Could he float? He had to relax. Maybe he could kick his legs and arms and make his way to the nearest bank. A number of water-soaked logs floated on the river. Maybe he could grab one and use it as a boat.

A boat. He felt a memory tug at his mind. What was it he was trying to remember?

Something floating down the river caught his eye. A blue rock glistening in the sunlight? It was coming towards him *against* the flow of the Frothing River.

A bright yellow slash of color appeared beneath the blue. The peculiar object was splashing the surface of the river with four — no, six — webbed feet. A large head lifted from below the waterline and a wide mouth opened to reveal jagged teeth. A deep cry sounded.

The hippoboatamus! The memory came back to Rupert. There it was, just as he had imagined it. Was it going to eat him? He tried to remember if he had dreamed up a yellow boat with a blue umbrella and six feet that ate people. He didn't think so.

He hoped it would reach him soon. He was losing strength, and his head went under water two more times. He was going to sink. Would he drown? Was this how it was all going to end.

The world around him went dark and silent as Rupert went under one last time.

Chapter 16

The End at Story

"Rupert, open your eyes," came a voice in the dark. A hand was patting his face. Flashes of light flickered.

Then all was blue. *Bright* blue. Was it the sky? No. It was a blue umbrella. Weaver smiled down at him.

"Remind me to teach you how to swim," he said, helping Rupert to sit and leaning him back on a cushiony seat.

Weaver was soaked and looked as tired and worn as Rupert felt. Looking around, he discovered he was aboard the hippoboatamus, and they were making their way down the Frothing River.

"What happened to you?" he asked Weaver.

"We were separated at the exit. It was closing. I pushed you out. I had to tear open a hole with my bare hands. I swam out and spotted you fighting for your young life. Then this bugger appeared out of nowhere. Any idea where it came from?" Weaver asked with a coy smirk.

Rupert smiled with a hint of pride and tapped his temple.

"Amazing," Weaver muttered to himself. "Never seen anything like it. Not even in the museum. My Quix would be proud to Imagine such a creature."

"Are we going at a proper speed?" came the tuba-like voice of the boat. Rupert looked up to see the face of the hippoboatamus peering back at them.

"Speed is fine," Weaver said. "Take us to Story. You'll find a small wooden pier on the eastern shore. And we can lose the sun umbrellas. Warmth will do us good."

"Very good, sir," the boat replied.

The umbrellas folded themselves up and vanished off to the sides of the boat on thick tentacles. The warm sun poured down on Weaver and Rupert as sunlight liked to do.

"Sun should dry us good," Weaver said, holding his face up to the sky. "Should be in Story in two hours."

"Actually, in two hours and ten minutes, at the current rate of speed, sir," the hippoboatamus corrected.

Weaver smiled.

"Rest, Rupert. You've had a busy day, and we haven't eaten lunch yet."

Rupert nodded and closed his eyes. The warmth on his face and the smell of the fresh air was better than any dream he had ever dreamt.

❈

The sound of hundreds of shovels obediently digging dirt filled the courtyard. The wingers patrolled atop the surrounding walls, many of them looking bored. They always hoped for a disobedient child to discipline. They drooled for any attempt by the children to use their imaginations. The wingers loved nothing better than instilling fear into young hearts to kill such powers.

Fancy's little arms ached. Standing in a hole that started five feet above her head, she filled her bucket with soil. Quix peered down.

"Take a break, Fancy. You look exhausted."

"I can't. It's not break time. They're watching. They'll scream and scare me and throw dead rats in here."

"Just pretend to work," Quix whispered. "Or let me come down there and fill your bucket."

"I don't want your help," she spat back with a wicked glare.

"What's the matter? Sounds like you're mad at me."

"How could you, Quix? How could you help that terrible monster?" Fancy's eyes filled with tears, and her bottom lip quivered.

Quix frowned and ignored the winger that was staring his way.

"I have to, Fancy. You're too young to understand. He's not as bad as you think."

"He's a monster. Dad will be so disappointed in you."

"Listen to me, Fancy. I have to do what I have to do. I'm the head of our family while we're here. I won't have my baby sister telling me what I can or can't do!"

"Hush! Get to work!" yelled a winger, who sounded more interested in the lump of filthy fat he was chewing on. "Or there'll be no water and slop for you!"

Quix threw the beast a look of disgust then turned back to his sister.

"Listen, Fancy…"

She ignored him and continued filling her bucket.

"Look at me!" he ordered.

She looked upward with a pout.

"I will help Murkus do whatever he wants. He's right. Imagination has destroyed Far-Myst. We'll be better off without it."

"Quix! Come over here at once!" a winger cried. Slog stood a few yards away with Xerks. "Milord needs you."

"I have to go. You do your digging, and be sure to rest your arms and drink all the water you can."

She looked at her feet.

"I love you, Fancy," Quix whispered, a tear filling his eye as he turned and joined Slog and Xerks.

The lair of Murkus was filled with steam rising from drums of water scattered around the room. The dark lord held a stone up to his mouth and blew a long stream of blue fire until the rock glowed whitish-red. He tossed it into a container of water at his feet. The stone sizzled wildly, and more steam rose.

Murkus reached into the small cave in the wall and came out with the rotting egg. He lifted it, with great reverence, level with his eyes.

"My sweet one. Feel the warmth and the comforting moist air. Just for you. Just for you, my little love," he said, gently kissing the egg. "You will be my child and be taught the ways of our proud heritage. There will no destruction in your world. No Imagination to attempt an end of our line. My son. My daughter. Whatever you are, your world will be ruled by the Dracoleens on great seats of our own power!"

Murkus took a seat on his throne of excrement and held the egg in his cupped scale-covered hands.

"They will all pay for what they did to our race, the traitors and villains!"

His head snapped to attention. His tail rose high, ready to strike. There was a feeble knock on the door.

"Enter, Slog! One more meek tap, and I will hang you like a door-knocker."

The door opened with a squeal of hinges, and Slog leaned in.

"The gardener and the strange boy are making their way down the Frothing on a rather—excuse the expression, milord—a rather Imaginative craft. They should reach Story by late afternoon."

"Bring me Quix and Xerks. And get two wingers ready to transport them."

"If I may, milord, they are here. I thought it best to be on top of things. With all you have on your mind."

Murkus shot a wicked glare at him, but then it softened.

"A rare show of initiative and smarts from my meek lackey! Bring the child ones in."

"Come in, wingless drones!" Slog ordered, feeling a tad more confident in the face of Murkus's rare compliment. "And pay your respects to your lord!"

Quix and Xerks entered and were shocked by the humidity. Quix's eyes went straight for the egg in the giant's hands. Xerks smiled and took a deep breath.

"I love thick humidity. It smells like adventure," he cried.

Murkus's reptilian mouth deformed into a frown.

"Hush your tones, boy thing!" he ordered but then, again, softened. "Much adventure awaits you. Here, however, speak softly. The Dracoleen egg must be revered."

Xerks bowed. "I am sorry, My Lord Murkus."

Murkus nodded and turned to Quix with a coy smile.

"Your tree-loving father and his new son are making their way down the Frothing. Traveling in a figment of the boy's twisted, devious mind."

"They are both traitors. We will do with them as you please," Quix said with his chin raised.

"Good lads! I have a great ally in you. My wingers will transport you to Story. You will arrive before my enemies. You will spy on them until you can eliminate the gardener and befriend the boy. But I caution you. He is more powerful than he himself realizes. Proceed with caution or the two of you may end up on the bottom of a muddy bank because of his Imagining."

"We can handle this pretender!" Xerks bragged.

"This is no pretender, my cocky-minded minion! It would serve you better to treat him not as an equal but as a superior!"

"Don't fret it, milord," Quix assured him. "This boy will be treated as if he were an equal to your mighty self."

"Let's not get carried away," Murkus said with a smile. "But I appreciate your attitude."

Slog stepped forward.

"Shall I call for the wingers, m'lord?"

"Yes, Slog. I want these two settled in Story before our pigeons arrive. You'll find the town to be rather quiet. My loyal wingers, shall I say, *moved* the residents to another town. One closer to me."

He stood up, and Quix and Xerks watched as his massive form stepped to the opening in the wall and gently returned the egg.

"Remember, my boys, I have eyes all over Far-Myst. Remove any thoughts of betrayal from your colorful young minds."

"We serve only you, my lord," Quix vowed with a bow.

"Murkus will rule Far-Myst!" Xerks cried, pumping his fist in the air.

"How charming," Murkus muttered. "And perhaps I will let you join me in a very special feast."

Slog took both boys by a shoulder and led them to a far wall. He slammed his fist against it, and a door slid open to reveal a cage. In the cage were the Seven Pigments, bathing in the nasty glow of shadowlight. The once-brilliant colors of the porkers had faded like those of painted toys left for years in the rain.

Xerks cheered and pumped his fist, and Quix shook his head disbelief.

Both Rupert and Weaver slept as the hippoboatamus cruised down the Frothing. Aside from early spring, when the melting snow flowed down from the Feigns, the Frothing River tended to be calm and smooth.

When Weaver finally opened his eyes, he looked across to the riverbank. He frowned and sighed hard. The trees and shrubs that lined the western side were colorless. Only gray leaves and pine needles waved in the breeze.

"It's spreading."

Rupert woke up and took in the view. He was also saddened by the sight.

"That storm is getting closer, too, isn't it?"

Weaver looked skyward. Wisps of black clouds, like smoky eels, swirled across the blue sky, bringing with them hearty gusts of biting wind. Washes of ripples raced across the face of the river, and the hippoboatamus rocked gently.

"How much farther until we get to Story?" asked Rupert.

"Twenty minutes," Weaver guessed.

"Nineteen and a half," the hippoboatamus corrected.

"We can have a real meal when we get there. I'm sure you're tired of jerky bark."

"It's not so bad. Better than splage."

Weaver took a waterbustle from his pack and offered Rupert a drink, but he refused. He had had enough water.

They rode in silence for a while.

"Do you miss your parents?" Weaver asked softly.

Rupert nodded. "My grandma, too. Do you think your friend will know of a way to cure the coffus?"

"I don't know. I hope so. My friend in Story is a very resourceful man. Was one of the Twelve many years ago. Name is Summit Wonder. He may have some ideas about getting you back to Graysland as well."

Quix and Xerks peered down in awe, the air rushing over their faces and holding back the stench of the wingers that held them firmly in their clutches.

"Look at that, Quix. The color is draining away. That whole section of forest is gray," Xerks cried out with great enthusiasm.

"Just goes to show how powerful Murkus is. No one else would dare steal the Seven Pigments," Quix said. He pointed down at the shimmering ribbon that snaked between the gray section of forest and the colored. "There's the Frothing. Story is on her shore."

"We are gonna be famous, Quix. We'll be the only humans to be written of as heroes in Dragon lore! What color pig ribs do you want?"

Quix smirked. but then his face grew serious. Xerks turned back to him.

"Just think—when Murkus's child is born, we'll be his equals. Two members of his inner circle."

"Child? What child?"

"The egg! You saw the egg he was keeping warm, didn't you?"

"The eggs of the Dracoleens are brilliant gold. Like honey," Quix explained softly. "That egg is black and brown. Rotted. Dead. Murkus hasn't accepted that."

"Hush with such talk, or I'll drop you both into the Frothing, you stinking little things," his winger threatened.

"You will not!" Xerks spat back. "We are the favorites of Murkus. He'll have your head for lunch if you lay one of your dead-rat fingers on either of us."

"Rotten maggot," the winger muttered.

Down below, a rectangle of wood appeared on the eastern shore of the Frothing. A patchwork of small houses and plots of grass and flowering trees sat beyond it. The wingers adjusted their flight muscles and began the descent.

Xerks's mouth widened into a smile of exhilaration as the sudden drop tickled his stomach. He yelled with great excitement as they sank down, down, down to the tiny town of Story.

They would arrive, as Murkus had told them, a couple of hours before Dream Weaver and Rupert Starbright. Then, they would wait. Patiently wait in the quiet little town of Story.

To be continued...

ABOUT THE AUTHOR

A filmmaker and writer since childhood, MIKE DICERTO has directed numerous shorts, music videos, documentaries, promotional videos and two feature films (*No Exit* and *Triptosane*). His first novel, *Milky Way Marmalade*, received rave reviews and won the the 2003 Dream Realm Award for speculative fiction ebooks.

Mike has many interests, including yoga (practicing for more than ten years), gardening (loves growing chili peppers in his rooftop garden), playing guitar (and trying hard to get better), cats (long-time volunteer at NYC's Ollie's Place Adoption Center and cat whisperer), really good and really bad movies and '70s TV as well as archeology, ethno-pharmacology, and all kinds of geeky and bizarre stuff. He is a dedicated MST3K fanatic. He thinks of music as his religion — especially classic rock.

He lives quite contently in a NYC apartment with his wife and soul mate, Suzy and their rescued kitty, Cosmo. He is very excited about the release of the first of his exciting new Rupert Starlight kid-lit series, which begins with The Door to Far-Myst.

ABOUT THE ARTISTS

BRAD W. FOSTER is an illustrator, cartoonist, writer, publisher, who has won the Fan Artist Hugo a few times, picked up a Chesley Award and turned a bit of self-publishing started more than twenty-five years ago into the Jabberwocky Graphix publishing empire. His strange drawings and cartoons have appeared in more than two thousand publications, half of those science fiction fanzines.

He spends huge sections of the year with his lovely wife Cindy showing and selling his artwork at festivals and conventions around the country.

CHRIS CARTWRIGHT is a computer artist who uses 3D programs and paint programs to create her works. Although she creates covers for any type of story, her favorites are fantasy, sci-fi and horror. She originally became interested in web design, which she went to school for, but after taking some art classes, found a new passion.

*Just when everything seemed
to be going right...*

Chapter 1
A Calm and a Storm

The rest of the journey on the hippoboatamus was
calm and uneventful. By the time the town of Story's
docks appeared, clouds had blotted out all of the
blue sky, and rain was falling hard. The two umbrellas had been raised again, and Rupert and
Weaver sat beneath their cover.

The hippoboatamus drifted up to the dock, circled around to line up with the pier and, with a bit
of strain, lifted its heavy body. There were pools of
water on the wooden surface from the downpour.

Beyond the pier was a narrow street lined with
small houses. Not a single light burned in a window nor did a single footstep splash a puddle. A
lone street lamp shone with yellow oil-fire, lighting
the wet cobblestones with a soft glow.

Weaver and Rupert stepped from the hippoboatamus onto the dock. Their clothing, which had
dried in the warm sun, was quickly getting soaked
again.

Weaver looked about.

"Seems oddly quiet, even for Story."

"How far away does your friend live?"

"Just a short walk," Weaver said, adjusting his pack. He turned to the hippoboatamus. "Thank you for the ride."

"Yes," Rupert agreed. "Thanks."

"You are quite welcome. Please Imagine me again should you need transport," the large creature replied then simply dissolved into the air and was gone.

Rupert looked at Weaver and tapped his temple with a smile.

"He's up here."

Weaver smiled back and headed off, his bootsteps joining the rain in breaking the silence. Rupert walked beside him.

The stones that paved the narrow twisting streets of Story were rubbed smooth as glass. Oddly, they were not slippery, even wet with fresh rain. The homes were all made of shaped stones and had been built with great care. Rupert noted that some of the doors were wide open, and in the front yards of others there were tools scattered about, rusting in the rain.

"That's odd," Weaver noted. "Folks of Story are not known for being so careless with their belongings. Tools are kept in tool sheds, and doors tend to be kept closed when it rains."

"Seems kind of early for everyone to be in bed," Rupert said.

"You're right. Seems more like everyone has left."

A chill raced up Rupert's spine. Why would everyone leave?

"Come, let's see if my friend is home."

Weaver hurried his pace and led Rupert down the main street and onto a very narrow side alley that wound up to the top of a small hill. At the end of a narrow lane sat a two-story home made of deep red stone and capped with a roof of blue wood. A round stained glass window was set above three regular windows.

The door was made of hammered brass, and on it was a knocker shaped like a hand holding an Illuminor, backed by the image of a majestic mountain peak skillfully stamped into the metal.

"This is Summit's home. That's his emblem on the door."

"Doesn't look like he's home."

"Let's have a see."

Weaver stepped through the front gate. He tapped on the door. The sound bounded down the lane like a skipped rock. When there was no reply, he tried again. Nothing. Again.

Weaver tried the doorknob. It turned, and the door swung open. To Rupert's surprise, Weaver entered.

"It's okay, Dullz. It's an unwritten rule amongst Illuminorians. Our houses are always opened to each other."

Rupert followed him in.

The home was simple and cozy. The furniture was handmade of deep-red wood, and a large fireplace was in one corner of the room.

Weaver called out, "Anyone here?"

There was no reply.

"Let's get that fireplace busy."

He retrieved some wood scraps from the fire closet and made a little tent of kindling. He took a small silver rod that sat atop the mantel and held it out to Rupert.

"This is a special device. A spark-lighter. Imagined by Summit when he was a child. Watch."

Weaver flipped a small lever on one end of the rod, and a glowing cloud of energy swirled around his hand. The energy condensed onto the rod and crept to the top end, where it burst into a small yellow flame.

"That's pretty good. In Graysland, we just have matches — these wooden sticks that light into fire when you strike them on walls and stuff."

"Sounds a bit dangerous. Must set a lot of houses on fire."

"No. But my mother always yells at me if I play with them."

"Your mother is a smart lady."

Weaver set the kindling ablaze, and in a matter of minutes, the room was lit up by the roaring hearth. After a quick search, he had found enough canned food for a hearty meal of beef stew and sugared carrots that he cooked on a special oil stove in the small kitchen. For dessert, they enjoyed sweet meekimeeki pudding, made from a fruit that sizzled and tickled your tongue with millions of tiny bubbles.

It was all a wondrous feast for Rupert's mouth, and for a little while all was great with the world. His cloths were dry, his belly full and his mind had calmed and cleared.

After they ate, Rupert examined all the paintings and artifacts that decorated the room. Over the mantel was a large portrait of a man with smiling eyes and a head of snow-white hair that fell to his shoulders.

"Is that your friend Summit Wonder?" he asked.

"No, that's his father, Rain. He was a famous artist. All of these paintings are his. That's Summit's mother, Melody." Weaver said, pointing to the lovely portrait of a serious-looking woman with beautiful long black hair and elaborate silken headwear. "She was a musician. Played for the Royal Orchestra that tours all around Far-Myst."

Rupert stepped up to a large shield that sat atop a wooden chest. On the bronze relic was the number 12. He turned to Weaver.

"Why did you quit the Twelve?"

"I'd had enough of people's squabbles. I wanted my children to be influenced by only positive things."

"I thought the Twelve *were* positive?"

"The Twelve were all good folk. Smart, dedicated men and women. In recent years, though, as things became more and more peaceful in Far-Myst, folks started becoming more and more unkind to the Truseens."

"Why? I thought they left and went somewhere else?"

"They did, but folks can be funny. Sometimes when things are good they try to find bad things even where the bad things don't exist. People started making the Truseens seem like some great enemy that was going to storm back into Far-Myst and make us all their slaves."

"Were they?"

"Nonsense. It was just stories dreamed up by boring-headed dolts who had nothing better to do. The Truseens were happy where they were."

"How do you know?"

Weaver looked away a moment then pointed to the paintings on the wall.

"Summit's father was also Truseen. Moved on to live with them. Summit would visit every so often and tell me stories of the mystical lands of the Truseens. He fell in love with a Truseen woman and married her. I learned that the Truseens are good folk as well. It was all just a difference of how people wanted to live. I got tired of the rumors."

"So, you became a gardener?"

Weaver smiled and nodded. "I grew to really love the solitude of the gardens. Especially after Celestia's death."

"Your wife, right?"

Weaver nodded. He drew the Illuminor, and it came to life in a display of sparkling colored light.

"This was hers."

Rupert's eyes widened. "Your wife was one of the Twelve?"

Weaver nodded and smiled with great pride.

"Yes, she was."

Across the road from Summit Wonder's home, two shadowy figures hid within a thick hedge. Quix and Xerks were spying. When they saw the lights of the Illuminor flash, their eyes widened, and a devilish smile crawled across Xerks's face like a bunch of insects.

"There they are. An honest-to-goodness member of the Twelve and his runt companion!" he sneered. "Let's kick the door down and rush them. Get the element of surprise on our side!"

"Didn't you listen to anything Murkus told us?" Quix snapped. "We have to handle this with care. We have to assume that boy has power."

"If you're too queasy, I'd be honored to deal with him myself," Xerks offered, gesturing to the knife that hung from his belt.

Quix grabbed him by the collar and glared at him.

"That'll be *my* honor. Do you understand me, Xerks?"

"Yeah, yeah. Relax. I'll take care of wonder boy."

"We are gonna make friends with him like Murkus ordered."

Xerks frowned but then agreed with a half-hearted nod.

⚙

"Celestia and I were the first married couple to ever serve as members of the Twelve. She was very skill-ful but could often be rash in her decisions. She was always a very impatient woman. That's what killed her."

"Was she in a duel? Or a battle of some sort?" Rupert asked.

"No. She was on a training mission. We had just celebrated Fancy's first year with us. Fancy was adopted—I found the little angel in a basket by the waterfall pines, wrapped in a white blanket with a rose on it.

"That's her name—Rose. I called her my Fancy Rose. Then it became just Fancy." Weaver smiled wide as his thoughts filled with images of his little girl.

"Even as an adult, Celestia had some use of her Imagining powers. We are trained to never use them in dangerous situations. Only the children can fully harness that energy. It often fails adults. Celestia used her Imaginings to build a bridge to cross a chasm in the foothills of the Feigns. She could not stay focused. It faded away, and she fell."

"I'm sorry," Rupert said, and meant it.

"Thank you, Rupert. That's why I was so against your using your own abilities. I wasn't confident of them. I'm sorry I yelled at you for using her Illuminor. No one but she and myself have ever held it.

"You were very brave to put yourself in danger with those black moths. That saved my mind—those things have the power to make a man daffy. Turn you into a walking dead man who fears his own shadow. Thank you, Rupert Starbright."

"You're welcome, Mr. Weaver. I don't think I was even thinking. I just did it."

"That's how courage works. A hero is just a person who acts out of desperation to save his or another's life. If you'd thought about it too much, you would have run for the hills like any sane man."

Rupert smiled and yawned wide.

"Will we make it to Flowseen tomorrow?"

"We should. It's a good half-day's walk from here. Much of it is, unfortunately, uphill."

"Great," moaned Rupert, rubbing his sore legs. "But at least you'll be free then to do more important things."

"Getting you home safe is important, Rupert."

They locked eyes, and Rupert felt a lump form in his throat.

Weaver looked away.

"Anyway, you must be exhausted. You can sleep in the bedroom—its at the top of the stairs. I'll sleep on this chair. We'll need a solid night's rest."

"Okay. Is there a bathroom?" Rupert asked, standing up.

"There's an outhouse. Around back."

Rupert headed for the door, and Weaver called him back. He was holding out the Illuminor.

"Here, Starbright, take this with you. In case you have a run-in with one of those moths."

Rupert was surprised by the gesture.

"Are you sure? It's your wife's."

Weaver nodded. Rupert took the very special dagger in his hands and nodded to him.

"Thanks."

"Make some noise before you enter—rabbicoons like to hide in there. They scare easy but can bite if you corner them."

Rupert nodded and left the house.

The rain was nothing more than a fine mist that felt nice on his face. He looked up at the sky and noted a few of the brighter stars were shining through breaks in the clouds. He hoped morning would bring more sun and warmth.

He walked along the neatly manicured path of gray and white stones that led to the door of the small structure he thought looked quite a bit like a phone booth back in Graysland. He tapped on the door a couple of times to scare off any animals hiding inside.

Without warning, someone grabbed his shoulders and threw him up against the door of the outhouse.

"Hello, there, wonder boy," a boy rasped in his ear.

Rupert tried to speak, but a hand was over his mouth. He tried to struggle free, but his attacker's strength was too much. Another, taller boy leaned close to him and sneered.

"What are you doing here?"

Rupert's mumbles were incoherent. The second boy gestured to the first to remove his hand.

"I have to go," Rupert innocently answered.

"You're coming with us."

"Well, what have we here?" his captor said as he freed the Illuminor from Rupert's grasp.

"Give me that!" Rupert demanded.

The hand went back over his mouth.

"Shut up. So, a future Knight of the Twelve with his own special dagger."

"I'll take that," the taller boy said, reaching for the Illuminor.

The other one pulled it away.

"Finder's keepers, Quix!"

"I said I'll take that!" He yanked the dagger away. "Let's go."

"What about the other one? Shouldn't you go in and take care of him?"

The one called Quix nodded.

"Take this one to the crossroads. I'll tend to the gardener and meet you there."

"And don't try anything funny, puny one," the wild-haired boy threatened with a wicked, green-tinted smile. "I have a sharp blade filled with powerful Imaginings. It'll turn you into a rotted rat if I choose. I am not afraid to use it."

"Could you at least let me pee first?"

"No."

"Let him," Quix ordered.

The other one frowned.

"Hurry up." he said, pushing Rupert toward the outhouse. "And no tricks."

Rupert stepped into the small structure and closed the door behind him. Quix grabbed Xerks by the shoulder and spun him around angrily.

"Fool! We were suppose to befriend him!" he said, trying to keep his voice down. "Now he'll never trust us."

"Relax, Quix. We'll use the old good guy, bad guy routine. It'll keep him off balance."

Quix sighed hard and gave in.

Rupert tried to overhear the conversation, but only muffled whispers made it to his ears. He had to think of something. His parents had taught him to never go anywhere with strangers, even ones his own age.

There was only one thing to do—he would slam open the door and make a mad dash back to the house. He had to let Weaver know what was going on.

"Hurry up in there!" the shorter boy ordered.

"Just a minute," Rupert replied.

"Let the boy do his thing, Xerks," Quix said. "Give him a minute."

A minute was more than he needed. He grabbed hold of the doorknob, took a deep breath and pushed the door open as hard as he could.

"Weaver!" he shouted as he threw himself past the two boys and raced down the path to the house.

"Hey!"

Rupert's heart was pounding as he came closer and closer to the door. Quix and Xerks were on his tail. He pushed open the door with his shoulder and entered.

"Weaver!" he shouted again. He entered the living room. Weaver was not there.

"Mr. Weaver!" he called, looking in the kitchen. Only dirty pots, empty cans and jars greeted him. He heard the door close then two sets of footsteps. He stepped back into the living room.

Quix and Xerks stood with arms folded, smiling.

"So? Where's your friend?" Xerks mocked.

Quix's eyes were darting about the room.

"Where is he?"

Rupert swallowed hard. *That's a good question. Where, indeed?*

(Follow Rupert's further adventures in Far-Myst in the exciting sequel **The Secret of My-Myst,** *coming in March 2012 from Zumaya Thresholds)*

38197241R00116